CLOUD DREAMER

JOHN ROWELL

ISBN: 978-1-923289-02-4 (Paperback)

A catalogue record for this
work is available from the
National Library of Australia

Cover Design: John Rowell and Clark & Mackay
Format and Typeset: John Rowell and Clark & Mackay
Published by John Rowell with assistance from Clark & Mackay

Proudly printed in Australia by Clark & Mackay

CONTENTS

AUTHOR'S NOTE

This novel is a work of fiction that was inspired by real-world events. Names, characters, businesses, organisations, places, and events are either the product of the author's imagination or, where real, are used fictitiously without any intent to describe actual conduct. Any resemblance to actual persons living or dead, events, or locales is either coincidental or historically correct. The spelling used is UK English, except where Czech diacritical marks for names and locations are employed to maintain integrity. Any mistakes are my own.

The moral right of the author John Rowell to be identified as the author of this work has been asserted.

NOTES ON THE CZECH LANGUAGE

Unlike English, where the pronunciation of words can change, Czech is phonetic, meaning pronunciation is consistent. This is all very well, but the refiners of the language have thrown in a number of diacritics: special marks that alter the pronunciation of some vowels and consonants. These look (and sound) daunting, but I have included them to preserve the integrity of the narrative.

English-speaking readers can just swim through these without worrying, but for those interested, these are a few of the diacritical marks and the changes they make to the pronunciation of words. So, **í** and **á** put emphasis on the vowel and stretch it out. For consonants, **ř** becomes 'rzh', **c** is 'ts', but **č** is 'ch', while ž sounds as 'zh'. If **s** is altered, **š** becomes 'sh'.

If it sounds tricky, it is; a bit like English speakers attempting French for the first time! Czech is complex, rather like its history, and I hope readers will forgive the writer for trying to take them a little further into the realm of these fascinating people.

ACKNOWLEDGEMENTS

I am enormously grateful to Stanislav Jircik, without whose memories and anecdotes on living in Czecho-slovakia this story of a life would never have been born. My good friend and mentor Dr Robyn Colwill provided valuable feedback on many aspects of the writing process. I also owe debts to friends in the Czech Republic who showed me so many places and told me of their histories on my frequent trips to that country. Jan Macola and Pavel Jiras, then working at Barrandov Studios in Prague, were extremely helpful in guiding me around this vast complex, including the sound studios and the enormous backlot. I have been inspired by several novels and writings on Prague and its history, but Richard Fidler's perceptive examination of the Czech people, their history, culture, and politics in his work *The Golden Maze* proved enlightening. Many thanks also to Jason Smith and the Clark & Mackay publishing team for their invaluable support.

CHAPTER ONE

'Out!' the chemist shouted. 'Get out and don't come back until you can remember what it is you are supposed to be doing!' Madame Rabasová glowered at the girl from under heavy black eyebrows, her white chemist's dust-coat barely concealing an ample bosom heaving with indignation. 'You are supposed to be concentrating when you make up customers' prescriptions. It's very important!' She thumped the polished mahogany bench for emphasis, making the large glass apothecary jars rattle. Blažena stood frozen in shock for a moment, then she turned quickly to prevent the chemist seeing her tears welling up. She shed her dust-coat, threw it on the counter, and fled the pharmacy. The tiny brass doorbell's tinkle mocked her as she ran.

She seethed as she ran to pick up her bicycle, leapt into the saddle and pedalled furiously, anywhere in her blind fury away from the pharmacy. She had never wanted to work there, only doing so at the urging of her stepmother Helena Kalinová, who was determined to find a respectable occupation for a young woman of eighteen years. A formidable woman, Helena had, of course, won out and had committed her to a life Blažena considered a drudgery. She nursed the suspicion that her stepmother had acted out of spite rather than for her stepdaughter's future.

Helena had never taken much interest in her step-daughter, who she regarded as an unwanted presence in the home. All her affection had been reserved for Miroslav, Blažena's father. Miroslav was a gentle man who basked in the light of his second wife's affections, and usually did as he was told.

Blažena hated the pharmacy's dark interior, with its great heavy cabinets and their innumerable little drawers, all meticulously labelled. Reluctantly, she had to memorise all those labels, and then also commit to memory their contents and characteristics, and how to mix them in the correct proportions for particular ailments. She abhorred the smells of those chemicals and compounds. Was this how her life was to be lived, mixing and doling out tinctures and folded paper packets of ingredients over the counter to customers who were, for the most part, disagreeable?

The image of Milada Nejedlová loomed in her thoughts. It was customers like Nejedlová who tested Blažena's patience to the hilt. Extremely overweight,

Nejedlová turned up regularly at the pharmacy, complaining loudly that the antacid powders she bought were not strong enough. Blažena couldn't bear the woman. *If you weren't constantly eating, you wouldn't have so much trouble with your digestion!* Blažena gritted her teeth on these occasions, yearning to tell the woman her opinion, but of course politeness won the day.

For its part, the pharmacy was on the better side of Rakovník's town square and almost opposite the charming Town Hall, which was chocolate-box pretty in delicate pink with its window framing and arches picked out in deep salmon. On its façade, the town's unusual coat of arms—a red crayfish—had become part of the place's heritage. The square itself was wide and long, with shady trees and garden beds ablaze with summer bloom. Husovo Náměstí, to give it its official title, was the second largest in Czechoslovakia, as Rakovník's inhabitants would announce proudly to any strangers they encountered.

Even though Rakovník was a relatively small place, it usually had a good number of visitors passing through, mostly on the way to visit the famous castle of Křivoklát, not far away. It attracted interest as one of the important Czech castles, and had been a royal seat for centuries. But on their way, visitors could see that Rakovník had a charm of its own, and the square definitely was a feature.

One end faced Saint Bartholomew's Church, with its separate medieval belfry protected by a wooden shingle roof. Colourful decorated shields on the shuttered belfry walls proclaimed its history, and it was famous throughout the country. The setting, adjacent to one of the town's two ancient gates, was the stuff of picture postcards. The charm of the church end of the square vied for attention with beautiful Art Deco and Baroque restaurant and shop façades at the opposite end.

No—Rakovník was nice enough. Her father's house was up from the square in a gracious street featuring a building faced with sgraffito—a decoration where figures were formed by scratching away a coating, leaving a contrasting colour beneath. Bearded warriors glared at each other across a curved window while above, Samson tirelessly battled the Philistines and fought his lion barehanded. It was considered a fine architectural feature, and often commented on by visitors to the town.

It was life in her father's house that constrained Blažena. Thanks to her stepmother's influence, it lacked any feeling of a true home, which she felt should be welcoming and loving. Her father was mostly absent for his work, which took him away for days at a time, leaving her to Helena's indifference.

It was so unlike life in former times, before her mother Ivanka had died. With her death, love had seeped out from Blažena's life apart from her father's muted support, and her work in the pharmacy only added to her misery.

Even though Ivanka had died when Blažena was very little, she still had vivid memories of her beautiful mother. Ivanka had been blonde, with sparkling blue eyes, and to Blažena she seemed to glow with a radiance. She was always there should Blažena fall or hurt a finger, and her patience and loving care never failed to take the pain away.

Then there was no-one to help take the pain away. Helena was a remote, stern person who could not be bothered with a young stepdaughter. She had been a reluctant parent, seeming only too happy to insist that Blažena should find employment when she was old enough to do so.

'Why not let her find something that she likes?' Miroslav had suggested once. 'Is it really a nice place for a young girl to work in?'

Helena scoffed at what she saw as Miroslav's leniency. 'What? And let her laze her days away while she dreams of something fantastic? I think not! She's of an age when she can be working and bringing some money into the household.'

So it was that Blažena was forced into the pharmacy, and into an occupation that only increased her resentment and animosity towards her stepmother. These feelings just boiled over at the chemist's criticism of her work, and were the reason for her bursting out of the shop.

Blažena made her way without thinking, anger and frustration lending strength to her pedalling, through the ancient gate, oblivious to the surrounding beauty and almost unconsciously out of the town limits and in the direction of the Berounka River twelve miles away. It was a long way to ride, but well worth it for the beauty of the river and the peace of the surrounding thickly forested areas.

* * *

Blažena stopped cycling and laid her machine down. Here all was light and airy, with a gentle breeze wafting the perfume of wildflowers and lush grasses. A verdant meadow spread like a broad undulating carpet leading down to the river, which ran through the town of Beroun itself, some few kilometres away. The part she had chosen narrowed to a series of small shallow rapids—the result of a little weir built across the river—and the splashing of water over rock provided a gentle curtain of sound before the river widened into the distance.

The river was diverted close by, in the form of a narrow stream leading to a little water wheel connected to a building once used as a flour mill. The mill was no longer in use, and the old wheel had ceased to function long ago.

In her imagination, Blažena could see it as it once was. She could see the mill-wheel revolving slowly, sparkling water falling from its paddles. The wheel's shaft would be turning, its clacking wooden cogs connecting to the stone that would yield the fine flour as it rotated—the whole scene viewed through a haze from the flour dust.

All was quiet now, and the little building was home to an elderly couple who farmed a small plot nearby. Blažena thought it a romantic setting, and sometimes chatted to the friendly owners, who were perfectly happy to live such a simple lifestyle.

The first time she came there, the old woman had waved to her and called out, 'Come in and have a coffee!'

Blažena had been a bit reluctant, but sought to be polite, and she was pleasantly surprised at the cosiness of the interior. There was a good wood-burning stove for cooking and heat, and rugs and throws for comfort in cold weather.

'I'm Magdalena and this is Lukas,' the woman said, indicating her husband. 'We've lived here for some years.'

Blažena was curious. 'Why did you come here? It's very isolated.'

'We lived in Křivoklát,' Magdalena said, 'and our son lived here as the miller.' Her expression saddened. 'But the demand for flour dropped off in this area and he moved away for work, and we just liked the peace of this area.'

Blažena recalled that first conversation and agreed entirely, because here she could escape the stress of her hateful occupation. *That gloomy shop*, she reflected. *Those obnoxious medicinal smells. That overbearing Madame Rabasová.* Here she could lie on a grassy slope, listen to the tinkle of water, watch the drifting white clouds cast their shadows over the countryside, and let her imagination run free. Blažena's eyelashes brushed new forms into the clouds every time she opened her eyes.

As they changed shape, they became for her objects of fantasy—now knights battling dragons, now fair maidens yielding to the knights' amorous advances, now a romantic galleon crewed by roistering pirates sailing through a cerulean sea. She saw herself as a princess, or even a queen commanding her celestial subjects. *If it were possible, I could be anyone I chose*, she thought drowsily.

In fact, Blažena could be any of her imaginary people. She was an exceptionally beautiful young woman with a perfect figure; her dark blonde hair and blue-grey eyes with a faraway gaze only intensified her allure. The more often she came here and the more her imagination led her into a world of fantasy, the more resolved she became. She couldn't endure the claustrophobic life in the chemist's shop forever. Somehow, something must direct her path to a different life. She felt that she could be good at something, if only she could discover just what that something was.

Another shadow passed over her, interrupting this reverie, and she became sharply aware that this was no cloud. She opened her eyes wide in fear as she focused on a figure—a male figure towering over her.

CHAPTER TWO

Blažena leapt up in alarm, folding her arms across her chest defensively. Her mind was a turmoil of fear. Why was she so stupid? She was miles from anywhere, and there was no way the elderly couple would hear her if she cried out. She stepped away from the man cautiously. 'Who are you? What do you want?' She was determined to keep her voice steady, even though she was trembling inside.

'I'm sorry I frightened you,' the stranger replied, his brow furrowed in concern and looking less threatening now. 'Were you asleep? I'm sorry if I woke you.'

'No—I wasn't asleep,' Blažena retorted in an attempt to defend her seemingly odd behaviour. She felt her confidence returning and explained, 'If you must know, I like to relax and gaze at the clouds, with their shifting shapes.' She realised how peculiar this must sound, as the stranger was looking at her intensely, his lip curled in a half-smile.

Reluctantly, Blažena thought he even looked attractive; he was tall, with light brown hair and piercing blue eyes. She guessed his age as not being much older than hers. He was casually but smartly dressed with pleated fawn slacks, a soft blue shirt and a light brown jacket.

He stepped back and gave her a small bow—an old-fashioned, gallant gesture which allayed her unease somewhat. 'My name is Radek Novotny, and I'm here with my colleagues.' He gestured into the middle distance, where Blažena could see a group of people, some vehicles and equipment. 'We're making a motion picture, and we're using this beautiful country area for a scene.'

Blažena's curiosity wrestled with her fear. She had seen a motion picture only once before, when a group had brought equipment into Rakovník and set it up in the Town Hall. It had been a short comedy shot in the standard black-and-white film, with jerky action and it was silent, apart from the musical accompaniment of a pianist who matched the erratic images on-screen with his playing. The pianist had to compete with the clattering of the primitive hand-cranked projector as he endeavoured to keep up, and his efforts were almost as entertaining as the on-screen proceedings. Even so, Blažena had been caught up with the rest of the audience as the flickering images transported them all into another world.

Curiosity got the better of her. 'What sort of picture are you making?' Her memory flashed back to the screening in the Town Hall. 'I've only seen one, and it was a humorous one. Well, everyone was making big movements to show how they felt, and there were signs from time to time showing us what was really happening.'

Blažena looked at him directly. 'What are those called?' she asked bluntly.

'Well, the acting has to be a bit exaggerated, because we don't have sound yet in motion films, and the signs are called "intertitles", so the audience understands exactly what's going on.' He shrugged. 'We hope to have talking pictures in a few years, but in the meantime ....' Radek spread his hands hopefully.

'As to your question,' said Radek, giving her an appraising look, 'we're hoping to make a drama, or more correctly, a melodrama.' Blažena took in the beautiful surroundings of the river with its grassy banks and the leaves of the nearby linden trees fluttering and bowing in a courtly dance to the measure of the breeze.

'It's not a very dramatic area,' she countered, 'where's the drama?'

Radek gestured down the sloping grass to the riverbank with its tall grasses and reeds. 'Well, in this scene, a beautiful young farm girl is running away from her pursuer, and the only avenue of escape for her is a small coracle floating near those tall reeds.'

Blažena could just make out the coracle, a clumsy-looking small craft almost circular in shape, with a single paddle lying across it.

'Escape,' she muttered, 'it doesn't look very safe for an escape.'

Radek's grin was reassuring. 'Oh, it's quite safe, and her escape will be very dramatic.' His expression grew serious. 'The only problem is, we don't have our farm girl for this scene.'

'Why not?'

Radek shrugged. 'We were supposed to meet our actress in Rakovník this morning, but she never arrived. To avoid wasting our time completely we're reviewing the setting, but we may have to pack everything up and return to Prague.'

Prague. Blažena had never been there. To her, it was the Golden City, —the City of a Hundred Spires—a magic place and one she could only dream of. She had seen pictures in books, of course, and it all looked like a fantasy city where wonderful things could happen.

In her mind's eye, she saw her favourite retreat, the nearby Berounka River, rippling its placid way through woodlands and later surging past giant rocky outcrops to eventually join Prague's mighty Vltava River. With some effort she abandoned her reverie and forced her mind to the present.

'Can't you find someone else?'

'It's very short notice, and none of us knows people in this area,' Radek gave her an appraising look. He shuffled his feet, looking rather like a guilty schoolboy. 'That is, unless you would be willing to stand in for her, just to gauge how the scene goes? It's an enormous favour I'm asking, I know, but we would be very grateful to you.'

Blažena's heart leapt, but then she realised the futility of the idea. 'I couldn't possibly. My stepmother wouldn't allow it, and anyway, I wouldn't know what to do.'

'Perhaps we could talk to her. We're a legitimate film company, even if we are very small. We call ourselves Pragcine. As for acting the scene, you would only have to take my direction. And—I really don't like formalities. Please call me Radek.'

Radek sounded so persuasive that Blažena's resolve weakened. 'My name is Blažena—Blažena Kalinová. You can try talking to my stepmother, I suppose, but she's a very hard woman, and we've never had a good relationship.'

Radek's smile was disarming. 'Let's try, anyway. I'll bring one of our cars over. We can load your bicycle and find out.'

Once they reached Blažena's home, it went just as she feared it would. Helena flew into a rage and accused Radek of leading her stepdaughter astray, and of putting wild ideas into her head. Helena was a tall woman, with golden hair and dark blue eyes now flashing with anger. Nothing a tearful Blažena said would soften her.

A very calm Radek endured Helena's tempestuous accusations. It was his mention of payment for Blažena's participation that tipped the scales. Helena's avarice won out, and she gave her grudging assent. Not only that, but the presence of a motor vehicle was a rare sight in Rakovník, and Helena preened at the stir it was causing among her neighbours. When Radek presented his business card with a small bow, it lent such an air of respectability that Helena's opposition shrank to nothing. To Blažena's eyes, it even looked as if Helena was flirting slightly with this handsome stranger.

While Blažena changed her working clothes into something more suitable for a virgin in distress, Radek promised Helena to return Blažena later in the day.

'We'll see you later this afternoon,' he promised.

'We'll have enough light to shoot,' he said as they drove away. 'It's still summer, and the light lasts very well.'

Blažena could barely contain herself as they neared the forest area. Would she be too nervous to perform? Would they think she didn't look appropriate for her role? She had picked out what she thought might be suitable to wear, and had chosen a white peasant blouse, a full floral-patterned skirt and an apron with a coloured fringe. Now she folded her hands over the apron and tried to take deep breaths to calm herself.

Once back at the location, Radek took charge, directing the camera operator to move his bulky camera on its sturdy tripod closer to the river bank in order to follow Blažena's flight down the sloping meadow and to the waiting coracle by the reeds.

'Now—' Radek switched into director mode. 'When I give you my cue, you run down the slope and look back as if someone is pursuing you. Then, when you reach the coracle, get in carefully and paddle away.'

Blažena thought this was not too difficult and, on cue, imagined her stepmother was chasing her. This helped her get into character and she fled down the slope, looking back in agitation a few times as she ran. When she reached the river bank, her skirt became caught up in the reeds and she hastily freed it. When she reached the coracle, she stepped in with great care, knelt down and paddled furiously.

All went well until she felt that her knees and her dress were becoming wet. She looked down and saw with horror that the coracle was taking in water. She shrieked with terror and tried to paddle back to the bank, but only managed to steer the craft into deeper water.

The waterlogged coracle started to wallow alarmingly. Blažena was just about to shout again when she lost the paddle. The unwieldy craft gave one final lurch and capsized. She tried to grab it but the coracle eluded her grasp, and she felt her world grow dark and silent as she sank beneath the surface. In the murk Blažena felt she could see her mother waving to her, and she stretched out an arm and opened her mouth to call the vision, but only bubbles came, and then she panicked and swallowed water. She was drowning.

CHAPTER THREE

Blažena's world became cool and dark, and she entered a dreamlike state. No thoughts, only the cool dark like a comforting blanket, when suddenly, she felt her peaceful journey into darkness interrupted by sudden rough jerking to her body. She could hear distant, agitated voices.

'Blažena! Blažena! Wake up!' The voices were louder now, close to her ear. She moved and vomited water. 'Sit up!' commanded the voice nearest her, and she tried to sit up. Her senses returned to her, and she realised that she was on dry land, and shivering uncontrollably.

'Blažena! Are you all right? Can you hear me?' The voice was Radek's, full of concern. She nodded weakly.

'Yes, I can hear you,' she muttered, shivering. 'What happened to me?'

'The coracle overturned and tipped you out, and you nearly drowned. Thank heavens you're all right.

The cameraman and his assistant dived into the water and brought you out.'

Blažena was still shivering from cold and shock, even though someone had found blankets to cover her.

'We must get you out of those wet clothes.' Radek again. Hands helped her up and across to the vehicles, where someone trawled through spare costumes and produced something suitable.

Sylvie, one of the girls in the film crew, helped her dry off and change, and she began to feel more like herself.

'It looked awful,' Sylvie commiserated. 'How did you feel when it happened?'

'I couldn't believe it was happening,' Blažena's teeth were still chattering. 'I just felt very cold, and everything went black.'

Sylvie rummaged in the back of the van. 'Here's some coffee,' she offered it to Blažena. 'I hope it's still warm.'

'Thank you,' Blažena sipped the coffee and began to feel more like herself.

Radek came up to her. 'We were so worried, but we got you out in time.' He had the grace to look slightly ashamed. 'But we kept filming and, apart from your accident, it looks like the scene went very well. In fact, your escape was more dramatic than we had planned! You have a natural talent.'

Blažena remained silent, reluctant to accept Radek's compliment. One part of her wanted to be proud and excited, but another part was resentful at the danger they had put her in. Her resentment bordered on real anger, and it was only through some force of will that she managed to stay silent, rather than let loose with accusations about how she had been treated in such a cavalier manner.

Radek acknowledged her coolness, no doubt feeling guilty about the whole misadventure. 'But now, we have to return you to your stepmother and face the music,' he murmured, 'which no doubt will be loud and tempestuous.'

She smiled inwardly. *Let him suffer a bit. It won't hurt him.*

* * *

The drive back to Rakovník was uneventful, Radek acutely aware of Blažena sitting beside him, glowering. She had every right to be angry, he considered. They had unwittingly put her life in danger, and it was only through quick action that she hadn't drowned. But it was while they were shooting the scene that still ran through Radek's mind. She had taken his direction quickly and intuitively, and had been totally convincing.

Radek could not know Blažena's thoughts as they drove, but as her anger cooled, she thought of the scene itself. She had followed Radek's direction easily, but the strange thing was, that when she began to move towards the water, it was as if another person had taken over her body, and she was actually living her.

Was this what acting meant? If so, she felt that she could possibly become a character and act and live as they would. The realisation dawned that this was something that she could do, and do well, even though this was only a kind of initiation. It was something Blažena felt that she could really focus on. She conceded that she was a habitual daydreamer, but this was possibly something that she could do to turn the dream into a reality. It would be up to Radek, of course, when they could discuss the matter afterwards. In the meantime, she maintained a dignified silence.

Eventually they arrived at Helena's house, preparing for another confrontation. However, this time it was different. Miroslav, Blažena's father, happened to be home. Normally he was at work, which took him out of town sometimes for weeks.

Miroslav was unlike his daughter in looks, with black hair now showing grey at his temples and a lined face which spoke of the stress from a hard-working life. His blue-grey eyes matched Blažena's, though, and now were wide with delight at seeing his daughter.

He gave a dubious look at the odd clothing she was wearing, but roared with laughter when Blažena and Radek recounted the day's events. Helena's expression was thunderous, but she had to take a back seat, since Blažena was the apple of Miroslav's eye.

Miroslav couldn't resist a small quip. 'So even though you tried to drown her, you really think this young daydreamer of mine can act?' He was incredulous. 'Besides, she already has a job in the local pharmacy!'

'Father, you know I hate working in that stuffy place!' Blažena and her stepmother had argued on this matter several times. Privately, Miroslav sympathised with his daughter but had kept silent on the matter.

Radek hastened to praise Blažena's performance, even though it had almost ended in disaster. 'Yes, Pan Kalin, absolutely,' Radek said, using the formal address. 'Blažena has an intuitive talent and, with proper training, I believe she could become an accomplished actress.'

Blažena held her breath. So Radek thought she had been convincing. *That means he thinks I can really act. It might mean I have a future in the craft.* Her heart soared.

Helena leapt into the fray immediately. 'It's out of the question,' she argued, stony-faced and implacable. 'Blažena couldn't possibly go to Prague. Who knows what might happen to her there?' She looked triumphant, as if her argument would brook no opposition.

To everyone's surprise, Miroslav spoke up. 'But doesn't she have a cousin living in Prague? Isn't it

Ludmilla? She could keep Blažena under her wing until she's established.'

Helena glared at her husband, but before she could unleash another tirade, Radek spoke up.

'What a good idea,' he enthused. 'Our company, Pragcine, is based in Barrandov, which we think will become a home for motion film production, and it's just across the river. Blažena wouldn't be too far from us, as we have an office in the city itself, and she would be quite safe travelling from her cousin's place. The Prague tram services are very good, too.'

Blažena had forgotten Ludmilla, but recalled playing with her when both were little girls. Ludmilla was slightly older and more sophisticated, but she had treated Blažena like a younger sister. Blažena couldn't envisage a better companion in Prague—if everything panned out well.

'Ludmilla lives in the centre of Prague, doesn't she?' queried Miroslav, 'so Blažena wouldn't have too far to travel every day. Besides, Ludmilla has a nice apartment as she works for the government.'

Miroslav was correct. The beautiful high plateau area of Barrandov was easily reached from the city centre by tram. It was said to be an increasingly popular suburb, with enterprising people having elegant villas constructed to take advantage of its height and splendid views.

Helena looked daggers at her husband. 'Well,' she said heavily, 'it looks like you have it all sorted out, but I still think it's a dangerous and foolhardy plan.'

'She will have Ludmilla's protection, I'm sure.' Miroslav looked placatingly at his wife. 'All we have to do is to contact her. I'm sure it will all work out. And, you know, it could be a great opportunity for Blažena.'

* * *

Some flurry ensued after the possibility of Blažena's moving to Prague. Radek and his team had returned to the city, offering to return to fetch Blažena if all went well with the arrangements. First, Ludmilla had to be contacted. Miroslav had requested a home telephone for his work, but suspected it would be a wait. In the meantime, telephoning meant going to the post office in the centre of town and using the telephones there. It involved using the cumbersome telephone apparatus, a wall-mounted box with a microphone and a corded ear piece. The lines were notoriously unreliable, and both Miroslav and Blažena had some difficulty with the connection and hearing Ludmilla when she eventually answered from her government office.

Blažena was overjoyed when Ludmilla's tinny voice announced that she would be happy to accommodate Blažena and help her get established in

Prague. Both were excited at the prospect of resuming their relationship after such a long period.

Helena chose to distance herself from any of the arrangements, and was frosty when Blažena and her father returned. 'You do this thing at your own risk!' she snapped. 'Don't be surprised if this all ends in disaster, and if it does, then don't come back here with your tail between your legs, because I wash my hands of you!'

Blažena quailed. What if Helena was correct and this was all a terrible mistake? Suddenly the enormity of her situation struck her. How to choose between a secure, albeit humdrum existence and the thrilling unknown of a new city, and a chance to test her intellect in the uncertainty of motion picture acting? She decided there was only one way to find out.

CHAPTER FOUR

Rain coursed down the bus windows as it lurched away from the Rakovník terminal on its way to Prague, the droplet-streaked glass reflecting its tears onto Blažena's face as she stared out into a gloomy afternoon. She had never been away from the place of her birth, and conflicting waves of excitement and sadness washed over her. Helena's farewell had been more of a dismissal than anything, causing Blažena to see her decision to leave as a momentous one.

Helena took Blažena's resolution to risk the safety of her employment for the uncertainty of any degree of success in Prague as a personal affront, and an act of wilful disobedience. She had unbent sufficiently to lend Blažena a suitcase—her oldest and shabbiest, dented and worn from years of use. It was her very unsubtle way of dismissing Blažena's decision as an act of the utmost folly.

Blažena smiled tremulously at her father sitting beside her. Rather than relying on Radek to come and pick Blažena up, Miroslav had insisted on travelling to Prague to support his daughter and to ensure her safety until she met up with Ludmilla.

'Do we stop anywhere?' she asked her father, partly to break an awkward silence, but also wondering how she would survive for over two hours on the badly surfaced roads.

'Only at Kladno, but at least it will give us a break for a little while,' Miroslav assured her, 'and we can walk around and maybe have a coffee.'

Kladno proved to be a dismal place, its prosperity mostly owing to the rich coal mines outside the city. At least they were able to stretch their legs before continuing the uncomfortable last section prior to reaching Prague.

* * *

Pulling in at Florenc, one of Prague's large bus terminals, was dispiriting. Florenc looked no better than Kladno, Blažena thought. At least the rain had stopped, giving way to a chilly afternoon with lowering clouds brooding over them as they descended from the bus. Large industrial buildings everywhere closed in on them like sentinels on the treeless streets. Blažena's heart sank. *Is this all going to be a dreadful mistake?* She was close to tears with fatigue and depression when she saw Ludmilla waving in the distance.

'Blažena! Uncle Miroslav!' Ludmilla's voice rang out from the far end of the platform.

'There she is!' Blažena's heart lifted at the sight of her cousin, and she and her father walked quickly to greet her.

'Blažena! How you've grown! And you're so beautiful!' High praise from Ludmilla, who was a lissome raven-haired beauty with sparkling dark brown eyes.

Miroslav stood back a little, savouring the reunion. He approved of Ludmilla, and considered her capable of mentoring his daughter in the capital. She was beautiful, sophisticated, and enjoyed a good position in the government service. Even better in Miroslav's eyes, was that from past experience he considered her utterly dependable.

'But I'm forgetting! You must be famished from your long ride here.' Ludmilla thought for a moment. 'I know what you need—a good coffee and a scrumptious cake—and I know just the place!' She piled them all and the suitcase into a nearby tram and they took off.

Blažena was giddy with excitement. Everything was so strange, especially the Prague trams with their bright red markings and angular pantograph arms clutching at the overhead electric cables, throwing off dramatic sparks every now and then.

The city seemed to beat to a faster rhythm than she had previously observed, the pedestrians walking more purposefully to their destinations. She noted with interest that their clothes were smarter, too, making them appear quite at home in the cosmopolitan setting. She realised that she would have to improve her wardrobe considerably to fit in. *Hopefully, Ludmilla will help me there.* The buildings became more attractive as they went, until finally they got out near a very impressive one.

'This is our National Theatre,' Ludmilla said, gesturing to it. 'Isn't it lovely? The style is Neo-Renaissance—I think.' She laughed. 'I'm no expert!'

Blažena had never seen anything like it before. Its grand colonnade was surmounted by classical robed figures while, further up, two groups of bronze horses strained at the leads of their chariots being driven by winged figures. The roof itself was decorated with beautiful gilt-trimmed finials. Words failed her and she stared, open-mouthed and trance-like, until Ludmilla interrupted her.

'We're not going there, though, but just across the road.' Avoiding the impatiently clanging trams, she steered them across busy Národní Street like a shepherd with a tiny flock, until they were on the steps of an imposing building. 'Welcome to Kavarna Slavia!' she announced grandly, and they entered.

Surprise piled on surprise for Blažena. Kavarna Slavia was a lovely café in the Art Deco style, its furnishing a mix of small round tables with bentwood chairs, larger tables and banquettes, and the whole interior lit by elegant ceiling and wall fixtures. Large windows gave out on one side to the Theatre across the street, and on the other to a magnificent river.

'That's the Vltava River, but look over to the right,' Ludmilla directed, and Blažena made out a large hill surmounted by elegant classic buildings and the towering spire of a cathedral. 'That's Hradčany,' she said, 'isn't it lovely?'

Blažena was speechless. Her mind whirled with all these new sensations. Maybe life in Prague would have the difficulties of the unknown, but there was no doubt that she had arrived at a marvellous place. Thoughts of enchanted fairy-tale castles crept into her mind, reminding her of those cloud fantasies by the Beroun River. Now however, this was no fantasy, and with some effort she brought her mind to the present, and to reality.

Ludmilla, meanwhile, had sought out an obliging waiter to store Blažena's single suitcase. The individual in question had at first been disinclined to perform such a lowly service, but Ludmilla's undeniable charm won him over, and he even helped them choose a table.

'First, though, you have to go to the glass counter over there and select your dessert cake.' Obviously, Ludmilla was an old hand at the Slavia. The choice of cakes took Blažena's breath away. *Home was never like this.* While they waited to be served, she wandered around, noting the many photographs on the walls.

Ludmilla noted her curiosity. 'They're all of different types—actors, singers, writers, political figures—lots of interesting and important people come here.'

Blažena was fascinated by all the images. Some obviously were studio portraits of actors and actresses, while others were of musicians, and she decided that the really serious expressions of some meant that they had to be political figures. *To think that all these important people came here!* Again, she had the impression that she had dropped into a different world.

Miroslav observed his daughter when she returned, starry-eyed. His heart gave a small lurch, and he realised that she wasn't his little girl any more. Her previous life was yielding to an as-yet-unknown existence. Miroslav was pleased, though, to note that Blažena approached her cake and coffee with relish, which he thought was a good sign.

'How is the coffee and cake?' he queried.

Blažena looked up and grinned. 'Like nothing I've ever tasted before,' she confessed. 'Everything about this place is unreal.'

* * *

Miroslav decided that it was the right moment. Drawing a small box from his jacket pocket, he passed it to Blažena. Inside was a beautifully chased gold heart-shaped locket on a chain. 'It was your mother's,' he said huskily. 'It's yours now. I hope it brings you all you wish for in life.'

Blažena couldn't speak. Her eyes pooled with tears as she clasped her father's hand across the table. Miroslav raised his head, his eyes moist. He knew that, in some way, he was losing his only daughter and it broke his heart, but he felt that this small gift might help maintain the loving bond they shared. His fingers fumbled nervously as he fastened the delicate clasp around Blažena's bent head. She raised her head, and gently touched the beautiful thing as if it were a talisman.

'You'll be all right here,' he said, waving a hand to encompass all of Prague. 'Ludmilla will keep you safe, and you can contact Radek soon, or wait for him to get in touch. In the meantime, you can discover something of Prague. When you do meet Radek, then you'll learn how your adventure will turn out.' He patted her hand encouragingly. Ludmilla smiled enthusiastically. 'Uncle Miroslav's right,' she said. 'You know I have a telephone thanks to my government job so you can call home, but more importantly, you can contact Radek.'

Blažena brightened, and her blue-grey eyes cleared to gaze lovingly at her father. 'That's right—I can keep in touch with you.'

Miroslav shifted uncomfortably in his seat. 'But now I really have to go, if I want to get home this side of midnight.' Ludmilla offered to guide him, but he sent her a warning look. 'It's all right—I know the trams to Florenc. You two stay here and enjoy the excellent coffee.'

He stood and Blažena rose to embrace him tightly. 'I love you,' she murmured, 'and thank you for everything!'

Miroslav hugged Ludmilla, and then was out of the door into the darkening evening to await his tram. If he had noticed, the National Theatre glowed warmly and the majestic Vltava flowed on its sparkling way, transforming the fairy-tale Hradčany into a thousand glittering jewels, but his mind and heart were elsewhere.

CHAPTER FIVE

Blažena's life took on a whirlwind aspect as Ludmilla took some time off to familiarise her with Prague. Ludmilla's apartment was in Bartolomějská Street, in one of the beautiful Baroque buildings that lined the cobble-stoned way with its narrow footpaths and ornate gas streetlamps. As it was located in the Old Town, most of Prague's beauty was within walking distance.

Blažena gawked like a tourist at the famous Orloj clock in the Old Town Square, and the elegant gold-en-spired Church of Our Lady before Týn. It reminded Blažena of the description of Prague she had read as being the City of a Hundred Spires. Now she was here, and she could actually admire them as they speared, gleaming, up into the sky. Ludmilla pointed out the house with beautiful sgraffito where the famous author Franz Kafka had lived. It resonated with Blažena, reminding her of that other house with sgraffito in her father's street, and she felt a momentary twinge of homesickness.

They sauntered across the medieval Karlův most, the iconic bridge built by the Emperor Charles IV, known as the 'Builder of Prague', and named after him. They traipsed up the steep hill to Hradčany, where they admired St Vitus Cathedral, and then wandered around the ramparts to gaze out over the beautiful city.

Everywhere one turned, Blažena thought, there was something to delight the eye—a lovely doorway, an elegant window, even a saint in a building's niche perpetually blessing passers-by. Seeing Prague was like looking through a giant kaleidoscope that revealed beautiful shards of history—fragments of centuries just waiting to beguile. Blažena was so delighted by it all that she almost forgot her purpose in Prague, but Radek's promise to contact her lurked in the back of her mind.

His telephone call came when least expected, and it was with some flurry that she prepared herself to meet again and to consider her future. His noisy Tatra motor car heralded his arrival, and they drove across the river up to the suburb of Barrandov. It was a lovely setting, high on a plateau, with elegant villas clinging to slopes that afforded stunning views.

'It's early days yet,' confessed Radek, 'but we have hopes that this will be the home of motion film in

Prague.' He gestured to a nearby building. 'Welcome to Pragcine!' Inside, the building was largely empty and had a partially glassed roof for available sunlight. 'We use natural light, and you can see the muslin screens we use to diffuse hard sunlight.'

He indicated large lanterns hanging from metal bars. 'Sometimes we need artificial light from these Klieg arc lamps, but they're a nuisance to control and irritating on the eyes.'

They went outside. 'We have an office in the city, but this is our set for filming,' Radek continued. 'We think others will set up here as well, thanks to Miloš Havel and his brother Vaclav, who've gained huge financial backing in all aspects of the film industry.' He gave her a direct, almost stern look. 'If you're really serious about working with us, I would put you on a holding salary while you study your first role. It would be the same character you played in the scene by the river.' Blažena just stared at him, speechless.

'Yes,' he said with a smile, 'we processed that reel and the results were excellent. You have what it takes!'

Blažena was puzzled. 'How can you tell?'

'You're intuitive. You reacted to the scene and created your character without thinking.'

Everything was moving so quickly that she almost panicked but secretly, in her heart, she was thrilled.

* * *

Some weeks later, she became more familiar with the business of film-making. Radek's patient coaching taught her how to move, gesture, and to use facial expressions and eyes for maximum effect. 'Don't forget pictures are silent at the moment, but soon they will be talking. In the meantime, you have to convey every emotion through your body.'

While she was absorbing technique, Blažena received some tips on make-up. Stefan, a cameraman, helped her.

'The film we're using now is sensitive to most colours except red,' he explained, 'so we have to compensate for that with make-up, not only on your face but on all visible parts of your skin. Hopefully, soon we'll be using panchromatic film, a new type that doesn't need much make-up at all.'

Blažena was surprised to learn that the odd tones of the make-up she had to use would help to make her appear natural on film. She was in a world in which fantasy appeared to be the norm.

'As for the actual film, we had been using cellulose nitrate film base,' Stefan continued, 'but it's rather unstable, and if not stored properly, it can ignite.'

Blažena looked alarmed at this. 'How do you get around that problem?' she asked.

'We can transfer our films on to cellulose acetate, a much safer film base, and we're now using that, and we make sure we store any older nitrate film safely.'

Blažena's mind whirled. There was a great deal to take in, both at the camera end and the acting process. She was disturbed that there had been an element of danger in the film used. Apparently, older film stock had ignited sometimes when being screened, posing danger to operators and audiences alike.

When she was able, she sat in on scenes being shot and studied other artists. She studied the effects of the different studio lights on actors' faces and bodies. She learnt quickly to avoid the novice mistake of glancing at the camera lens unless directed to do so, and began working with fellow performers. *It's not such a problem*, she reflected. *I can just become my character. I'm no longer Blažena.*

The sequence in which scenes were shot didn't necessarily follow the screenplay, and she understood that the final film would be edited from the several reels acquired. She found that the film she was working on dealt with a strong woman who managed to break from a bad relationship—a departure from the usually passive roles for women. The working title was *Escape from Darkness*.

Radek offered her a contract with Pragcine. 'You've worked hard, and now you're a member of the company.' She was taken aback when he asked what her screen name should be.

'Blažena—' She couldn't think. She didn't want her real family name for some reason.

'Why not just "Blažena"?' Radek smiled. 'It has a certain style, and it's easy to remember.'

When *Escape from Darkness* was finished, it gained cinema release and was moderately successful. Blažena was content with her screen name, and it was to remain throughout her acting career. During the months that followed, Blažena studied intensively to hone her acting prowess.

* * *

'I want you all here,' Radek announced, facing the crowded room in Pragcine's city office two years later, 'because we have exciting news.' The room's occupants, made up of administrative, technical and acting members of the company, whispered excitedly amongst themselves.

Radek continued. 'We have to make a major change to our technical and performing styles.' He paused. 'We're working towards a shift to sound in our films.' He waited until the animated chatter subsided. 'This will mean new practice with the setting up and disguising of microphones, and soundproofing of studios.

'We'll be using the new tungsten filament lighting instead of the old arc lights which were noisy and irritating. Most importantly, we'll be testing our acting company's vocal suitability for this new venture.'

Blažena eyed her colleagues with some concern. Their voices had not been an issue up until now. How would they cope? How would she? Up until now, she had not regarded her vocal instrument as being important to her work.

'We'll be using the more modern technique of recording the sound track optically on the edge of the film itself. That way, the sound will be perfectly synchronised with the picture.' Radek paused. 'I know that this is a lot to take in at once, but soon we'll be doing vocal tests, and once that is done, we'll proceed to our next film—our first talking film!'

'We have a working title of *Blue Diamond*. It will take some time to equip and set everything up, but we can do it. As some of you might know, another director, Friedrich Fehér, made *When the Strings Shriek* last year. It's the first Czech fully synchronised sound film, and if he can do it, we can too!' It was obvious that Radek was very excited about the new technique, but his audience seemed restless, trying to work out just what it meant in terms of the necessary vocal skills.

Everyone was nervous on the day of the voice tests. Blažena hadn't thought much about her voice, except that it was a low to medium pitch. She liked singing, and knew that she could hold a melody well. Maybe that would help. She just hoped for the best. *Oh well, I just have to see what happens.* She had felt so happy in Prague, up until now achieving in a field she had never dreamed of. One thing was for sure—she could never, ever go back to Madame Rabasová and the chemist shop in Rakovník.

One by one the actors took their places before the large round microphone set up on a table in the test booth. It stood like a metallic sentinel, round and gleaming, challenging each speaker. One by one they read the script provided. The men on the whole seemed happy with their results, and Blažena thought her test was adequate. She was relieved when it was approved. She noticed Marika, one of the younger actresses, crying in a corner. Blažena went over.

'What's the matter, Marika?' she asked gently, 'didn't you like the voice test?'

Marika sniffed and wiped her eyes. 'They said the microphone thing couldn't pick up my voice well. They said my voice was too high, and if I turned my head away just a little, my voice disappeared completely. I was frightened of the thing—it was like a giant eye, and it terrified me!' She was disconsolate. 'It means I can't do any speaking roles.'

Blažena tried to comfort her. 'It doesn't mean that you can't do something else, like non-speaking roles, or even working behind the scenes.'

Marika agreed, but remained subdued. 'I'll try to see what they can give me,' she said. 'I really like it here, and I don't know what else I can do.'

Blažena considered herself very fortunate. Only by a stroke of luck did she meet the film crew at the Berounka River, and only through Radek's diplomacy was she able to come to Prague and work with the company. *Like life itself,* she reflected, *the film business is a very chancy thing.*

CHAPTER SIX

Emboldened by the success of Fehér's come-dy-drama, filming resumed with the new sound equipment installed at Pragcine on Barrandov's hill. Other film companies began sharing the area, and it soon became a film-making enclave.

Blažena received voice coaching, which meant that the emphasis was now more on the dialogue and less on gestures to avoid being melodramatic. Radek schooled her in a more natural acting technique. She began to film *Blue Diamond* and to her relief, her vocal talent matched her acting abilities and, from the initial shoot, her subsequent scenes continued smoothly.

Elevated to the status of a leading player in Pragcine, her salary increased considerably. She was able to lease an apartment in the city not too far from Ludmilla's and near a tram stop for access to Barrandov.

She relished the new freedom even though she missed Ludmilla, but they continued to meet regularly over coffee. She even managed to have a social life, encouraged by Ludmilla. This enabled her to break from the cycle of intensive studying, coaching and filming. She began going to better clubs and even the odd party. Ludmilla was the prime mover here, as she had many acquaintances in the government.

Radek was the odd man out. 'You have another party tonight?' he demanded once. 'Be careful that your social life doesn't interfere with your work!'

Blažena sensed it was jealousy rather than the quality of her work that upset him. 'Don't worry—it won't. And,' she grinned wickedly, 'I'm learning new life experiences!'

Her social life certainly didn't affect her filming in the least, and she drew from both the real world and the shadow world of her vivid imagination to become a very versatile actress. This stood her in good stead when a great change came that affected Pragcine and its staff.

The much-anticipated scheme of creating a massive film production centre became a reality early in 1933. Situated in Kříženeckého Square, Barrandov Studios was an enormous complex designed by the famous architect and director Max Urban, and included stunning villas and even a restaurant in the precinct. To promote the importance of the studios, a shuttle bus brought guests and the curious from Wenceslas Square in the heart of Prague up the hill to admire the project, which featured three large sound studios.

Radek was ecstatic. 'This will be our future! Even if we combine with another film company, the resources here will mean faster production with better quality.' He was full of ideas for more films dealing with experimental themes and larger casts. It promised to be a new era for film-making, certainly in Prague, and possibly even the whole of Czechoslovakia.

His enthusiasm was infectious, and everyone looked forward to new, exciting projects. Blažena was caught up as well, although from time to time, she was experiencing a feeling that this was not everything in life. She was very satisfied with her work, and even enjoyed the occasional journey home to see her father and the indomitable Helena. Miroslav was even more proud than ever of his daughter and was captivated by her recounting of work and of life in Prague.

'How do you find life in Prague?' This was a surprise question from Helena, whose curiosity got the better of her. 'What are they wearing? What do they eat?'

Blažena took this as an opportunity towards healing the rift that she felt had always existed between them. 'Well, I have to wear the costumes designed for whatever film I'm working on,' she replied, 'but usually I wear what's current, and that seems to be influenced by the designs for the great Hollywood stars. Here, it's wider shoulders, longer skirts and generally more fitting waists. Fortunately, the handkerchief hem is out!'

Helena snorted. 'That's all very well if you're slim, but that doesn't suit everyone!'

'I know,' Blažena grimaced, 'and I have to be very careful to keep in shape for my roles.'

'And the food—what do you eat there?' Helena seemed to be living vicariously through Blažena's experiences.

'Oh, much the same as here, but more elegant presentation. And'—Blažena grinned ruefully— 'much smaller portions!'

* * *

Even though they didn't see each other as frequently, Ludmilla still regarded herself as Blažena's social secretary. She had even acquired a boyfriend, Alex, whom Blažena met one evening when they were having dinner at Café Louvre, an enormously popular meeting place once frequented by the famous Kafka.

'I'd like you to meet Alex,' Ludmilla said, indicating her dining companion. 'He's a publishing manager.' The handsome Alex had regular features, a sensuous mouth and intense blue eyes that absorbed the world around him. With wavy fair hair and an athletic build, he had a pleasant manner—a good counterbalance to Ludmilla, whose government job could sometimes cause her to be tense and nervous. Blažena was to find that Alex's mischievous grin and quick wit would never fail to get everyone in a party mood.

'Now all *you* need is a boyfriend!' Ludmilla pointed a perfectly lacquered finger at Blažena. 'Then we could all go out as a group, and you would have something else to think about other than acting!'

Blažena had smiled, but secretly she was annoyed. She had everything, didn't she? Youth, good looks, and a blossoming career in film. Surely that was enough? But, the truth of what Ludmilla had said struck home like a lightning bolt. Ludmilla was correct. That was the missing element in her life—she had not found someone to love.

She had focused so much on her profession and her career that it had become her entire world. A feeling almost of panic surged over her. How could she correct this anomaly in her life? Radek was dear to her but, even though they were very close, he was her employer and instinct told her that a romantic affair with a colleague courted disaster, and could spell the end of a promising career.

Blažena determined to address this missing part of her life, and resolved to enlist Ludmilla's assistance. After all, Ludmilla was a woman of the world—a career woman who had managed to meet a very suitable partner. That was it—she would entreat Ludmilla to introduce someone from her circle of acquaintances to her.

As it happened, things took on a brighter turn with an opportunity to meet more people. 'You'll never guess!' Ludmilla was beside herself with excitement one day, not long after a session at the Slavia. 'The department I work for is holding a dinner dance in a fortnight's time, and we all can bring a friend. You must come!' Ludmilla had all the details. 'And—' she paused dramatically. 'It's going to be held at the Hotel Steiner!'

Blažena regarded her blankly. 'What's that?' She had never heard of it.

'It's just the most elegant hotel in Prague!' Ludmilla exclaimed. 'It's only been open for a few years, and it's famous for its dinner dances. They're held in a special room—the Boccaccio Hall. The Steiner is right next door to Obecní Dům!'

With a little effort, Blažena conjured up the latter in her mind's eye. She recalled seeing Obecní Dům, the beautiful Art Nouveau style Municipal Building, located just off Na Příkopě, an elegant shopping street.

She thought this opportunity came as manna from heaven—an elegant evening's enjoyment plus the opportunity to meet not just one, but possibly several attractive men. Further, there was the anticipation and excitement in selecting an ensemble to wear. Serious planning was essential.

After much deliberation Ludmilla chose an elegant costume in midnight blue, more slim-fitting than was usually worn, with a dropped waist and longer skirt that set off her height and dark colouring. She decided on black accessories in keeping with her dark theme. Blažena debated whether to go dramatic like her cousin but, in the end, she settled for a silver embroidered powder blue dress with a fitted bodice and a pleated skirt. It suited her voluptuous figure perfectly. She would wear a silver fillet to highlight her dark blonde hair, and match it with silver accessories.

* * *

On the much-awaited day, the trio of Ludmilla, Alex and Blažena set off on a perfectly clear evening along Na Příkopě towards Hotel Steiner. Alex looked dashing in a light grey suit that set off his fair hair, and he wore what Ludmilla privately thought a slightly garish tie, but she conceded it matched his breezy personality. The women attracted some admiring glances from male passers-by, which restored Blažena's confidence, since she was feeling the odd person out in the group.

They joined the chattering throng moving towards the special entrance to the Boccaccio Hall and soon were inside. Blažena gasped. Ornate pillars supported elegant Baroque-decorated boxes, then soared up to a pediment of cupids against more gilt curlicues, which culminated in a domed ceiling with a glittering central chandelier.

'I can't believe it,' she whispered to Ludmilla. 'This is more elegant than any film set I've seen!'

'And just look at the crowd,' Ludmilla pointed out. 'Most of the department is here. It's as well we dressed the part, and—note the orchestra.' She gestured to the musicians in their formal dress on a small dais. 'We'll be dancing as well. Let's find our table.'

Alex immediately claimed Ludmilla for a dance while Blažena sat, taking in the crowd and thinking she could be in a scene from an elegant film, when she was startled from her reverie.

'May I have this dance?' He was tall—very tall. His black hair was slightly curly and, as Blažena rose, he held her gaze from under long dark lashes. His eyes seemed almost black, and they sparkled like jet. He escorted her out to the floor. 'You are very beautiful,' he murmured as they danced, and Blažena's heart gave a sudden lurch.

When the music stopped, he led her back to the table. 'I could have danced with you forever,' he said softly, his breath warm in her ear. 'We will dance again.' Then he turned and walked away. Blažena's eyes locked on his broad-shouldered, slim-hipped figure. Her heart sang with desire and lurched again, more violently this time. She had the strangest feeling. Was this just attraction, or was she falling in love?

CHAPTER SEVEN

Blažena could hardly contain herself until Ludmilla and Alex returned. 'I've just danced with the most amazing man!' She took a few deep breaths. 'But—I don't even know his name and he doesn't know mine!'

'Are you going to see him again?' Ludmilla looked sceptical. 'Maybe he was just flirting with you,' She frowned. 'You need to be careful with men—you can't always trust them, you know, and I'd hate you to be taken in by a handsome face.'

'I don't think so—he promised to dance with me again,' Blažena was hopeful. 'I think he'll keep his word.'

They both were waiting in an agony of suspense when Blažena's mystery partner appeared out of nowhere, bowed, and took her hand. Ludmilla's eyes opened wide at the handsome stranger.

'Don't look too hard,' Alex warned, 'or I might get jealous!'

They reached the centre of the floor. 'My name is Josef,' the dark stranger offered. 'Josef Kozel.'

'Mine is Blažena,' she replied. 'Blažena Kalinová.'

Josef studied her intently for a while as they turned on the floor. 'I have the feeling I've seen you before, but I don't know where.'

'On a poster, or in a cinema somewhere, perhaps?' Blažena teased, eyebrows lifted in amused query.

Josef's face cleared. 'That's it!' he exclaimed. 'You're in films—I recognise you now—you're the famous Blažena, the film actress!'

Blažena lowered her eyes demurely. 'Well, maybe not famous, but actress, yes,' she admitted. 'Now it's my turn.' She examined him, head cocked to one side. 'Accountant? Taxation?'

Josef grinned ruefully. 'Guilty as charged—accountant for the government, but I'm a real person, too. I like films and dancing, and I'm a passionate opera lover.'

Blažena looked dubious. 'That sounds—really interesting.'

'Oh, it is,' Josef was enthusiastic. 'Opera has wonderful music and singing, great costumes and staging. You would like the costumes and the sets, I'm sure. It's a bit like films in a way—it transports you into a completely different world.'

'Then I'm sure I would,' she conceded, 'and I'm sure it's wonderful.' She was determined not to spoil the moment, but smiled at Josef, gazing into those jet-black eyes as they danced.

* * *

Things moved swiftly from then on. Blažena and Josef met sometimes with Ludmilla and Alex, but mostly just with each other. Being together was difficult sometimes, as Josef had an occupation with regular hours while Blažena's filming could take place at any time of day or night. The separations put her into an agony of anticipation.

Ludmilla was eager for details, and couldn't resist interrogating Blažena whenever they had coffee together. 'What's he really like?' she demanded on one occasion.

'Well, he's very attentive, and also very courteous,' Blažena considered. 'And I like him very much.' She paused. 'I do have a concern about mixing a romantic relationship with my film career, but I think we can work things out.'

When they did manage to meet, they talked about things they had in common—likes and dislikes. Blažena was still not as entranced by opera as Josef, but let the matter lie.

'We don't know much about our families, do we?' she mentioned one time. 'My father's alive, but my lovely mother died when I was very young.' Her expression was sober. 'Then my father remarried, and my stepmother isn't so nice. What about you?'

Josef's face was expressionless. 'I lost my parents when I was quite young, so I suppose that makes me an orphan.' His expression lightened. 'But at least I had the good fortune to be brought up by a loving aunt. Aunt Berthe became both mother and father to me. I love her dearly.'

Blažena was sympathetic. 'That must have been terrible for you. How did you manage?'

Josef shrugged. 'I think I coped by withdrawing into myself. I was a loner as a child, and even now I'm not so much a sociable person. I get on well enough with my work colleagues, but my work enables me to function independently.' He grinned, and his jet-black eyes twinkled. 'Then I met someone wonderful who drew me out of myself!'

* * *

They walked one night after supper at Kavarna Slavia, along the river embankment and beneath the colonnade leading to Charles Bridge. It was a peerless night, with only a few scudding clouds against an inky-blue sky sprinkled with stars. There were very few people on the bridge, and they strolled slowly on the medieval cobblestones past the series of baroque saint statues. Josef stopped by the famous statue of St John of Nepomuk, according to legend tortured and then flung into the Vltava for refusing to reveal the Queen of Bohemia's confessions. They both leant against the balustrade, taking in the river below and the majesty of Hradčany above.

They stayed that way for some time when Josef turned towards Blažena and, in a husky voice, asked, 'Would you consider marrying me?'

She started and stared at him, wide-open blue-grey eyes into bottomless black. 'I will consider it,' she murmured, and looked thoughtfully down at the Vltava, glittering as it splashed against a great stone pier. Unconsciously, she fingered her mother's gold locket. To Josef, it seemed an eternity. She dropped her hand and then smiled impishly. 'I have considered it, and yes, I will marry you,' and melted into his embrace.

They remained like that for a while, each aware of their own turbulent thoughts. Blažena looked up at St John's head, encircled by a halo of golden stars. *An omen?* She wondered.

'Perhaps we should go back,' Josef murmured. 'You must be feeling cold.'

'No—I feel wonderful! Let's cross the bridge and then come back.' Blažena felt like she was walking on air rather than cobblestones, joy suffusing every fibre of her being. 'We should make this moment last.' And they walked on, two young people in their own world of dreams.

Word of Blažena's engagement spread quickly around the Barrandov Studios. Colleagues visited whichever set Blažena was working in to congratulate her. Radek was very happy for her.

'I hope this doesn't mean you'll stop acting for us.' His expression was concerned. 'Pragcine would be losing a major asset. Remember, you were a big hit in *Blue Diamond*.'

'Of course not.' Blažena's smile was sly. 'I'll want to have children sometime, you know, but I'll return to work if you still want me.'

'Naturally, we will still want you,' he replied with a smile, and so a pact was sealed.

* * *

At first Ludmilla was ecstatic. 'I want to throw an engagement party for you!' Then she frowned in frustration. 'But I'm going for a short holiday with Alex to Lidice.'

Blažena was curious. 'Why Lidice?' she asked. 'Oh—your parents live there, don't they? I remember my mother speaking about her sister Vera.' She sighed, conjuring up the memory of Ivanka, her own long-dead mother.

'Yes,' Ludmilla sounded very happy. 'I really love them, but I haven't been able to see them for quite a while, even though it's not far away, near Kladno.' She considered for a moment. 'I know—we'll have your party as soon as we get back!'

Blažena's engagement party was a huge success, with most of her Barrandov colleagues there. Josef rounded up some of his friends and accountancy colleagues so the evening was voted something of a crush, which made Ludmilla, as the architect of the celebration, very satisfied. After that, life went back to normal for everyone except Blažena, who was torn between her on-going film commitments and anticipation of her marriage to Josef.

* * *

Although things appeared normal in Czechoslovakia, there were murmurings of unease further away. Radek intimated these in a Pragcine meeting.

'There is discontent near our borders in the Sudetenland, where the people speak German. Apparently, they want to align with Austria, and if not Austria, then the German Republics.' He shrugged his shoulders and made a futile gesture, his hands wide with palms up.

'This, in itself, will not concern our business, but a more worrying series of events may threaten our country, even though President Masaryk's current government is stable. The real concern is Austria's Adolf Hitler, whose shrewd dealings have resulted in his assuming power as the German Reich Chancellor. He's very determined, and by what's going on, has an obsession with power.'

Blažena was unsettled by all this and discussed with Josef their decision to marry. He mentioned the not-so-subtle changes he had noticed whenever he went to Vienna for the opera.

'There seems a definite feeling of disquiet there, and people seem worried at how convincing Hitler's speeches are in the frequent Nazi rallies and parades in Germany. They're making very theatrical demonstrations of strength to either impress or intimidate the people. It's difficult to say at the moment.' Josef considered. 'Maybe we should marry while it's still calm.' Finally, they decided that they would marry in May 1935.

'I would like a lovely marriage for my lovely bride.' In his excitement, Josef was already making plans. 'The world should know how happy we are.'

Blažena was less enthusiastic. 'I'm not sure. It might be better if we just have a quiet civil ceremony and then go for our honeymoon.' She saw that Josef was disappointed, but reassured him. 'We'll have all our lives together, remember.' She kissed him gently. 'Nothing will part us.'

* * *

The die was cast, and their wedding party consisted of a small group. Radek, of course, was an honoured guest, as were Ludmilla and Alex. Blažena invited Miroslav, who came looking older but very happy at the honour of giving his daughter away.

'Helena couldn't come,' Miroslav said, looking worried. 'She says she's fine, but she's getting very thin and weak.'

'What does your doctor say?' Blažena was troubled.

'That's the problem—she refuses to go. I can't persuade her.'

Blažena resolved that soon after her marriage she would make a trip back to Rakovník to see Helena and try to help in any way possible.

Concern over Helena's health did not affect anyone else's spirits at the wedding party, where they enjoyed a banquet in a private room at Kavarna Slavia. Blažena felt that she had never been so happy, and resolved that nothing would mar the perfect relationship with her Josef—despite his ridiculous obsession with opera.

CHAPTER EIGHT

The canteen at Barrandov was full as usual, and buzzing with gossip. Blažena only half-listened, pondering when she and Josef could take their honeymoon around their busy work schedules.

'And now she's in Germany.' Lena, a junior actress, was full of news. 'She's not content to make films here; she has to go and work for UFA!'

Blažena was curious. 'Who are you talking about, and what on earth is UFA?'

'Lída Baarová, you must know her!' Lena couldn't wait to tell it all. 'She's the Czech actress who won a contest for a role with UFA in Germany. That's Universum Film AG, the biggest German production company.' Lena sniffed contemptuously. 'She got a part in the film *Barcarole*. And she only became popular when she bumped into Hitler, who championed her because she reminded him of his niece! Talk about luck!' 'But—' She paused dramatically. The word is, now she's become Joseph Goebbels' mistress! And—he's married with children!' Now she had everyone's attention.

Goebbels was known to be Hitler's chief propagandist for the burgeoning Nazi Party. He was a master of his craft, using any form of media available. Film was one medium he used effectively.

'Baarová needs to be very careful, then,' someone said. 'When Hitler hears about it, he won't be pleased that one of his senior Nazi ministers who's already married is having an affair with a Czech, with the Sudetenland issue building the way it is.'

'It probably won't do anything for her career.' Lena's expression was smug. 'She should have been patriotic and stayed in her own country!'

Radek had been listening to the conversation. 'Hitler is very much a concern,' he said. 'Since he was made Reich Chancellor of Germany in 1933, he's making moves to expand his power and influence. The Germans love him because he has helped forge a rapid economic recovery, and given the German people a renewed confidence and sense of national pride.'

'But isn't that a good thing for Germany?' Lena asked. 'It just means they are becoming more prosperous.'

'No, it's not that simple.' Radek was convinced. 'The Sudetenland issue is just one example of his desire to expand Germany's territory.'

He looked around the table. 'It's a long time now since the end of the First World War,' he said, 'but does anyone here know just what happened then?'

His audience looked at one another, but no-one was willing to make a guess.

'Well, after Germany surrendered, a treaty was drawn up by the victorious countries.' Radek frowned. 'While some reparation had to be made by Germany, it was especially harsh. It was contained in the Treaty of Versailles.'

One or two in the room nodded as if they could recall the time and decisions made then.

Radek placed his palms down on the table. 'That treaty was demeaning for Germany. She lost a lot of land, including the Sudetenland, important industrial land around the Rhine, and was demilitarised. Worst of all, Germany had to acknowledge full responsibility for the war, and incurred an enormous reparation debt.' Radek looked around questioningly. 'Can anyone understand how demoralising that was for Germany, and why it longed to recover its power and prestige? Oh, and remember that Kaiser Wilhelm was forced to abdicate and live in the Netherlands.'

He made a questioning gesture. 'Has anyone here heard of Hitler's *lebensraum*? No? Well, it means "living space", and that's just another word for "expansion", or if you want a more sinister meaning, try "invasion".' He made air quotes to emphasise the terms.

There were gasps around the table, followed by agitated conversation. Radek raised his hands for silence.

'Now, just think,' he said, 'Germany at last has a leader who is instilling national pride, is improving the economy—remember, the inflation rate in Germany after the First World War was catastrophic—and also happens to be extremely ambitious. Imagine what all that can lead to.'

Blažena was anxious. 'What might it mean for Czechoslovakia and especially for all of us here?'

'Nobody knows, but we might see dramatic changes in a couple of years.' Radek shrugged. 'So, we just have to wait and see.' Then he smiled. 'But—on the bright side, we're all here, and we can continue doing what we do best—make good Czech films!'

Privately, Radek was very concerned for the future of Pragcine and Barrandov in general. He had been speaking with Stefan, one of the cameramen. Stefan had recently come back from Germany with his assistant Ondřej Mudra, and had disturbing news to relate.

'There is more tension building over there,' he reported. 'But the big news is, Hitler has found a new talent—a woman.'

Radek was incredulous. 'How can that be, and who on earth is she?'

'It's very interesting,' Stefan shrugged. 'Apparently his new talent is a woman called Leni Riefenstahl.

She's a beautiful woman, a former athlete and dancer. An accident ended her sporting and dancing career, and took her to film acting, where she proved to be the perfect Aryan model. Apparently, Hitler was captivated after he saw her in some of the so-called "mountain films"—human against nature themes, all lederhosen and traditional dirndls. He saw her in *The Blue Light*, and was dazzled by her.'

'Yes, but what did that lead to?' Radek interjected.

'Well, there's much more!' Stefan was excited. 'This Riefenstahl has become a very talented film editor and director, and Hitler persuaded her to direct a film all about the 1934 Nazi Party Congress in Nuremberg. I managed to see it in Berlin, and it's technically brilliant. It was released as *Triumph of the Will*, and it's the most powerful propaganda.'

Radek's mind reeled. He had respect for the art of film, and his dream was to create films to entertain, move and delight his audiences. Now the filmic arts were being bent and distorted to control people's minds. He shuddered in disgust.

'But, what about Goebbels?' Radek was incredulous. 'He's supposed to be Hitler's chief pro-pagandist!'

'That's the most ironic part!' Stefan could hardly get the words out. 'Riefenstahl has complete autonomy over her work and answers only to Hitler, and—Goebbels hates her!'

$$* * *$$

With tensions building, Blažena and Josef decided to take their honeymoon in a lull period, rather than lose the opportunity altogether. They decided on Šumava, a beautifully wooded national forest area that would enable them both to relax and reinvigorate in the clean air and beautiful surroundings.

'If you don't mind, I would like to pass through Rakovník,' Blažena suggested, 'and that way I can see Miroslav and Helena.' She looked worried. 'I know Helena is ill, and I'd like to know more.'

Josef had no objection to the plan. 'That's fine—I can spend some time with Miroslav. I like him very much.' He was thinking aloud. 'We can hire a car, if we can find one, and go where we want.'

Planning accomplished, they set about organising tasks for their absence and packing for the trip, feeling as excited as children let out of school. This was a long time coming, and they couldn't wait.

Miroslav was delighted to see them, especially his daughter. He embraced Josef warmly, glad to have him in the family. Helena seemed happy to see them, but Blažena was horrified at how she looked. Helena had lost a lot of weight, and her face was gaunt. Her once-blonde hair was peppered with grey and her once-brilliant eyes faded. Blažena found an opportunity to speak with her alone.

'Helena, you don't look very well at all.' Blažena was concerned. 'Why haven't you seen a doctor?'

Helena shrugged. 'I know that a doctor can't help me at all, so I'm not wasting time, and I don't want to worry Miroslav even more.'

Blažena persisted. 'Are you in any discomfort?'

Helena shook her head, but even the slight movement caused her to wince in pain.

Blažena was determined to do something, anything, to alleviate Helena's obvious suffering. Helena had never shown her much affection as a stepmother, but Blažena saw it as her duty to help. While it was years since she had been to the chemist's shop, she made the trip once more to Madame Rabasová.

'Goodness, girl.' The chemist stared at her. 'What a beauty you've become!'

'Thank you, Madame,' Blažena took in the familiar sights and smells of the pharmacy. The memories of working there rose like bile in her throat. 'Unhappily, I've come on a serious matter. My stepmother is ill, and refuses to see a doctor. I know she's in considerable pain.'

Madam Rabasová was sympathetic. 'I can dispense a mixture which will help with the pain, but that is all it will do.' She busied herself with various ingredients. 'Here. She should take it when she feels the pain badly. But—she should really see a doctor.'

Blažena smiled. 'I know, but Helena is a very determined woman. I speak from years of experience!'

Helena was pathetically grateful to Blažena for the medicine. Her hardness had dissipated and Blažena was sad that so much else had been lost during those years of coldness from her stepmother, who now seemed reluctant to have Blažena and Josef leave them.

The married couple eventually set off from Rakovník on a fine morning, determined that this would be the best honeymoon, and worth waiting for. Even though the car they had found was rather battered, it helped provide a sense of adventure.

'I just want to walk in the forest, and follow little streams,' announced Blažena lightly, testing their compatibility.

Josef smiled. 'You can if you wish,' he said with a grin, 'but I want to walk in the open hills and take in the views.'

'It looks like we can't agree.' Blažena affected hauteur. 'But surely we can agree on what we'll do in our cabin at night?'

Josef just smiled wickedly. 'Oh, I think we'll come to an arrangement.'

And they did.

CHAPTER NINE

Blažena and Josef had decided that she would keep her apartment but live with him in his until they decided whether they needed a larger place. Josef's apartment was also in the Old Town, so they were not too far away from Ludmilla and Alex.

'Just because we're married, I don't want to lose touch with Ludmilla,' Blažena said. 'She's my best friend, apart from being my cousin.'

Josef agreed. 'That's no problem—I like Ludmilla and Alex a lot. After all, she was your bridesmaid, and Alex was my best man. We owe them.'

'Yes,' Blažena agreed. 'They supported us enormously. In a way, they were our family, because we had no-one in Prague to turn to. Your lovely aunt was no longer with us, and my father and Helena were too far away.'

Once the domestic arrangement had been sorted, both Blažena and Josef refocused on their work. Josef was studying for a better position in accountancy.

'It's a bit harder, working full-time and studying as well,' he reasoned,' but at the end of it all, I hope it will enable me to get a better position, and if I'm lucky, it will mean a salary upgrade. That will help us establish ourselves.'

Blažena was studying the screenplay for a proposed film, with the working title of *Enduring Love.* 'And I'm studying for a new film. If it comes about, that will mean another income from the contract. We're not doing so badly!'

* * *

All went smoothly for some months, until one morning Blažena felt unaccountably nauseous. *That's quite unlike me. She* searched her memory for what they may have eaten the previous couple of days. *I usually have a good digestion.* Unconcerned, she returned to the perusal of her screenplay.

It was only after several repetitions of the symptoms that suspicion dawned. She managed to get together with Ludmilla for a serious conversation.

'It probably is what you think it is,' Ludmilla was convinced. 'If you want to be sure, why not have a consultation with the film company doctor at Barrandov?'

Blažena was horrified. 'That means everyone will know!'

'They will have to know sooner or later,' Ludmilla reasoned, 'and anyway, you must tell Josef. 'And,' she added as an afterthought, 'you have to tell Radek. You're working on a new project, and you must be fair to him, too.'

Blažena was undecided. She saw the logic in Ludmilla's advice, but found it difficult to take the first step. Eventually, she plucked up the courage and made an appointment with the film company doctor. Doctor Tomek was a fatherly type, and one to inspire confidence.

'No doubt about it, my dear,' he affirmed after his examination, 'you are pregnant, and there is nothing wrong. Should you wish, you will be able to continue working, providing you don't do anything strenuous.'

Suddenly, Blažena felt an inexplicable frisson of fear. It must have shown on her face, because Doctor Tomek reassured her.

'It's all right,' he said. 'You're young and in perfect health, so you should come to term without any problems.'

Blažena thanked him and then pondered on her next course of action—when and how to break the news to Josef. She felt conflicted over the revelation. First, there was the implication of having a child on her acting career, which she loved. Then, there would be the impact of a child on their social lives. Above all, she was uncertain as to how Josef would react to the news, since they hadn't yet discussed having children.

One evening, over Josef's favourite meal of veal schnitzel and buttered potatoes with a side of cucumber compôte, Blažena told her news. To her surprise, Josef did not receive the news quite as she had expected. He seemed pleased, but nowhere as excited as she anticipated. Blažena put it down to the concern of becoming a parent. *After all, it's quite a responsibility to become a father for the first time. We're so lucky that we have managed to establish ourselves.*

'Will you keep working?' Josef thought that she should take things easy immediately.

'Of course,' Blažena laughed. 'I can keep working until I start to show, and I can finish the shoot long before then.'

'Are you sure? have you told Radek?'

'No, but I will tomorrow when I see him.'

Radek was hugely pleased for her in a way that Josef had not been. 'That's wonderful news!' He beamed. 'I know I'll lose you for a while, but you can finish shooting *Enduring Love* before then. Where is it going to be born?'

Blažena considered. 'I think I'll go home to Rakovník. Now that my father has managed to have a telephone connected to the house for his company, I can be in constant touch with Prague. There's a good midwife and doctor at home, and I sense that Helena would like to see the baby born, and'—she laughed—'I certainly know the local chemist very well!'

* * *

Blažena finished shooting on *Enduring Love* during the next few months and, towards the end of the year, made plans to return home in preparation. Josef was not so happy with the arrangement, but Blažena persuaded him.

'You can get time off around your study program and visit regularly and, near my time, you can stay at our home. I'm sure if you ask your supervisor, you will get the time off work, too. Remember, now we can telephone if you really have to be in Prague for something important.'

'We haven't discussed what happens after the baby is born,' protested Josef. 'What then?'

'I thought that I would return to Prague, and we could get someone to mind the baby when I go back to work. The apartment is big enough for a nursery, and we could be based where we work.'

Josef considered. 'I suppose that's feasible. We still need to work out if my apartment will fit three people, even if one of them is very small!'

'I know,' Blažena was conciliatory, 'but hopefully we can work that out later. We have the time.'

* * *

And time they did have. Towards Christmas, they took the opportunity to spend the chilly evenings exploring the beauty of Prague in winter. The crisp air took on a sparkle, glittering with the first gentle falls of snow. The ancient buildings softened under their snowy blanket, and streetlamps glowed more warmly, creating halos around them. Their golden light pooled onto the cobblestones beneath, picking out the tiny glittering snowflakes.

Store windows along streets like Na Příkopě were changed from their usual arrangements of wares for sale and transformed into magical settings with their displays of angels with trumpets, nativity scenes, toys and traditional foods. Children, bobbled caps pulled down and thick mufflers pulled up, crowded against each display window, their breath misting up the glass in their attempts to catch sight of the fairylands within.

The Old Town Square was festive, with its stalls selling all manner of delicious foods, and the air was heavy with the aromas of mulled wine, freshly baked pastries, roasted chestnuts, and crisp pork basted over charcoal braziers. People strolled about dressed in warm and elegant costumes, some pulled by their children to the series of stalls laden with delights. Everywhere, there was the sense of goodwill that the festive season brings. Blažena and Josef made the most of it, as they knew it would be the last Christmas before they, too, became a family.

* * *

Miroslav was delighted that his daughter was coming home to give birth. Even Helena seemed rejuvenated, aware of an increasing fondness for her stepdaughter, underpinned by a sense of guilt at her previous cavalier treatment of the younger Blažena.

Ever since Blažena had left for Prague, Helena had become acutely aware of the absence of Blažena's bubbly personality around the house. Added to this, her conscience pricked at the realisation of the indifference she had exhibited towards Miroslav's daughter. It left her with a sense of remorse, and she was hoping for a reconciliation of sorts. She had a nagging feeling that her illness might not allow her to make up for lost time, but still she was attempting to make amends.

'I've just finished it,' she announced proudly, 'and isn't it lovely?' She held it up for approval. The article in question was a knitted baby jacket, the last item in a layette Helena had been working on for months. All done in fine cream wool, it had been a labour of love for her.

'It's very beautiful,' Miroslav smiled tenderly. 'You're really looking forward to this little addition, aren't you?' He studied his wife. She had put on a little weight, and no longer looked as gaunt as she had. *Maybe the anticipation of the baby has given her a new lease on life.* Whatever the reason, Helena seemed more alive, and Miroslav hoped against reason that her health was improving.

'I don't know why, but I am.' She smiled at him. 'We never had any children, and perhaps this little one will be a gift of some kind. Girl or boy, it will be of your blood, and you must give it all your love.'

'No—we must give it our love together, and let's hope that we both live to see it grow up.'

Helena sighed. 'Yes—let's hope for that, whatever may happen.' She looked away, a shadow crossing her face. 'We only have so much time. We must make the most of it.'

Miroslav looked concerned. Privately, he wondered at Helena's apparent strength. She had improved since hearing the news of Blažena's pregnancy, and he concluded that it had to be strength of will that supported her, but could strength of will alone keep her alive to see the birth of her step-grandchild?

CHAPTER TEN

In the following year, Blažena's life was divided between her work at Barrandov and the prospect and preparation for her baby. Post-production on *Enduring Love* was proceeding well, and Blažena knew it would be completed some time in advance of her baby's arrival. She was pleased to be involved with the post-production, as Radek had indicated she could have some input into the editing of her scenes.

At first, Blažena didn't think she would be that interested in the post-production. Gradually, though, she became fascinated by the processes and the skilled staff involved. The primary—and mammoth—task was to edit the entire film from all the individual scenes shot. It all had to flow and make sense according to the director's and editor's vision.

Occasionally, Blažena had to do some studio voice dubbing where the post-production staff needed it. Then—and this was something she hadn't even considered—there had to be a myriad of other sounds inserted to make the scenes lifelike. Without them, she realised, the edited film would sound lifeless and artificial.

'It's amazing,' she confided to Radek. 'It creates such an ambience that really brings a scene to life. And the funny thing is, one isn't aware that it's there, but very aware when it's absent!'

Radek just smiled. 'It's all a part of the craft of creating the illusion of reality in film. We must remember that we're creating a kind of fantasy— another world that the audience must be persuaded to believe is real.'

Then there was the music. To Blažena, this felt like the icing on the cake. The composer had to create atmospheric music to suit the pace and emotion of the edited scenes, and to make sure that the music synchronised perfectly with the images. It was ages ago, she reminisced, from that early film she watched, spellbound in Rakovník, with the hand-cranked projector and the pianist frantically trying to play music to match the flickering images on the screen. *How far my dreams have brought me*, she mused, *and how far will they take me from here?*

Radek was happy with the film's progress and even had another project lined up for Blažena. He was excited about this one, which he saw as the ideal vehicle for her. 'It will suit you perfectly,' he enthused.

'You can really draw on your acting depth with this one—it's a heavy drama. We don't have a working title yet, but it will be a star-maker, I promise you!'

Blažena smiled. 'Why don't we take things a bit slowly? I've just finished *Enduring Love*, and already you have me in front of the cameras again!'

Radek had the grace to look shamefaced. 'You're right; it's just that I worry that after you have your child, you'll lose interest in acting, and where would I be then?'

'Don't worry,' Blažena reassured him. 'You know how much I love the work. It would take something calamitous to stop me from film-making!'

Even so, she had the underlying feeling that she might want to devote more time to her child than she initially expected. *Might I become so engrossed with my baby that I can't devote any attention to anything else? I know it's possible, but I must try to achieve a balance here.* That would jeopardise her future career, she knew. It would be an extremely difficult decision to make.

* * *

The cold winter days held their grip everywhere, with chilling sheets of rain, blinding sleet and treacherous icy streets making any attempt to leave the apartment a risk. Blažena no longer made the trip to Barrandov, as *Enduring Love* was complete and only awaiting its promotion and cinema release.

Josef was anxious about Blažena going to Rakovník. 'It's still bitterly cold, even though it's the end of winter,' he complained. 'Are you sure you will be comfortable at your father's?'

She nodded. 'I'm sure. The house is well heated, and it will be spring when the baby is due.'

Josef still wasn't convinced. 'Yes, but you know what a Czech spring is like—it's all mud and slush and weak sunshine. It's not healthy!'

'I know all about the winter—and the spring,' Blažena smiled, 'but I've got this irrational wish to have the baby in my old home. Maybe it's something to do with my mother.' She looked solemn. 'I do remember her, you know, from when I was little.' She paused, and her eyes took on a faraway look. 'I can even remember her making a kind of cake for me. Now I know it as a *koláč*, but then it was just a lovely light yeasty cake with lovely plums in the mix, and when it came out of the oven, she would sprinkle it with icing sugar and then cut it into squares for me to eat. It was so delicious.' Her eyes misted. 'Some memories are very strong. Maybe having my baby in our family home is a kind of homage to her, and strangely, Helena has become so sympathetic and motherly it's uncanny. It will all work out.'

'If you say so,' Josef conceded, 'but I'll take time off and come to Rakovník before it's due. I want to be there.'

Blažena took his hand. 'Thank you—that means everything to me.'

* * *

As she wandered through Rakovník's park, Blažena could see that winter was gradually releasing its icy grip on the land, and tiny wildflowers were silently heralding the first signs of spring. Crocuses struggled to raise their beautiful heads through the last snowy winter blanket, and the white drooping blossoms of snowdrops appeared everywhere. The snow was melting to reveal the rich earth, ripe for spring growth.

Blažena loved this time of the year, when nature's cycle would bring the dazzling fingers of the golden rain tree, together with the delicate hues of the lilac. She felt it was so life-affirming, and she knew part of the emotion she felt at the rebirth of the natural world was inextricably bound up with her child's approaching birth.

In Rakovník's streets, she encountered several of her childhood friends, and surprised herself by giving her married name of Kozlová without thinking. *Prague is a world away, and apart from being married, I might never have left here.* Rakovník was so quiet that it seemed to have no pulse. *How different from Prague, with its elegance and bustle and the stresses of film-making.* But the stresses, in hindsight, had brought her enormous personal satisfaction—a sense of achievement that she felt she could never have imagined. Her previous life in Rakovník had been so quiet that it seemed close to inertia—a film run in slow motion.

As she toiled up the narrow lane that led from the city square to Miroslav's house, it seemed that the present was the only world she desired. *But that's because of the baby—it's being home here and pregnant that's making me feel that I don't need anything more in life.* But a tiny voice whispered, *You know there's more to life than having this child, and you know full well you yearn for it. It's now in your blood.*

Josef came to Rakovník as soon as he heard that Blažena's time was coming. There was a lightness in the air. It was late April, and the days were lengthening, pushing back against the bleakness and chill of winter.

Blažena was overjoyed to see him after an interval of a few weeks. 'It's wonderful to see you,' she said as she embraced him. 'I can't wait until it really comes, and—I can't wait to lose the extra weight! I've become so heavy and clumsy; my balance is all over the place!'

Miroslav and Helena, too, greeted Josef warmly, overjoyed that they would be included in the birth. The house had been scrubbed from top to bottom, and the bright and cheerful room allocated for Blažena already had a tiny crib in anticipation.

A day or two before Blažena was due, the local midwife bustled in with all her accoutrements.

Marta Pribyl was a buxom, cheerful soul with much experience in the birthing of children. She radiated calm and confidence, for which Blažena was grateful. 'She's so good-natured,' Blažena confided to Helena. 'Nothing seems to be too much trouble.'

Helena smiled. 'But then, you're a very good patient. You will do everything she tells you to.'

'Well, between her and our local Doctor Svoboda, I feel very secure,' Blažena conceded. 'And I should be a little nervous—this is my first time!'

Blažena's labour was mercifully short, and then it ceased. A loud cry from a pair of strong little lungs heralded the entry of a tiny soul into the world.

Josef's face was a study. 'She's exquisite,' he said, gazing down in wonder. 'She's the most beautiful little girl—a Blažena in miniature. She looks just like you!' He bent his head and kissed Blažena tenderly on her forehead.

Blažena looked up at him drowsily. 'I'll take that as a compliment,' she said, smiling.

Miroslav's eyes misted up. 'She is beautiful,' he agreed. 'My gorgeous little grand-daughter.' Unashamedly, tears ran down his cheeks as he remembered another such time when his own tiny daughter came into the world, and he was able to gaze tenderly into his own wife's eyes.

Helena bent over the tiny creature. She teared up too at the beautiful child, but maybe her tears were for a child that she had not had, and could not ever have.

Blažena had never felt a happiness like this. It transcended every joy she had ever known, even falling in love with Josef. She had a momentary twinge of guilt at that, but she felt that now her world was complete.

CHAPTER ELEVEN

It seemed illogical that the natural order of things could change so much, but change they did. It was as if Miroslav's house had become the epicentre of the universe. And it was all because of a tiny creature with her incessant demands, which were instantly and lovingly met. Tiny Zdenka—for Josef and Blažena had decided to name her so—held sway over the household as if she were a princess, which in their eyes she was.

It was not only within the household that young Zdenka's power extended. Old school friends of her mother came to cluck and coo, Miroslav's friends arrived to congratulate him on his grand-daughter, and even Madame Rabasová deigned to visit, proclaiming the new arrival perfect. Radek clattered from Prague in his elderly Tatra to pay court to the new arrival.

'She takes after her mother, doesn't she? She's a beauty, too.' He grinned at Blažena. 'You do know that you're sorely missed up on the Hill—Barrandov, that is.'

While this adulation was flattering, it was also tiring for the household, and Blažena especially was grateful when the visitors thinned out after a few weeks, and relative peace reigned at last. 'No—you can't have it, naughty precious,' Blažena admonished the baby in her crib, when little hands tried to grasp her mother's gold locket, as it swung tantalisingly on its chain. She gazed down into large blue eyes. 'Not now, but later; much later, my love.'

Weeks passed, and Blažena realised that it was time for her to return to Prague, Josef and their apartment.

'Oh, no!' Helena was distraught. 'You can't possibly leave yet; it's far too soon.'

'But, Helena,' Blažena was concerned. 'This is all getting too much for you, and you know you aren't well.'

It was true. Helena had been tireless in her support of Blažena for all the baby's needs, but the effort was showing, and again she looked very drawn.

Miroslav entered the conversation. 'Blažena's right, my dear,' he consoled. 'You have been a tower of strength for Blažena and the little one, but it's taken a lot out of you.'

'It's just that—I feel—' Helena struggled to express her feelings, 'I feel that I won't see either of them again!'

'Nonsense!' Blažena attempted to be positive and confident. 'We'll visit often, and then you'll see how much little Zdenka will have grown, never fear.' Over Helena's bowed head, she looked at Miroslav, and he returned her gaze with his own—doubt and sadness writ large.

* * *

At first, life in Prague was unsettling. Blažena had become used to the tranquillity of Rakovník, and even the baby sensed the difference in surroundings. Josef and Blažena had discussed the advantage of having someone to mind little Zdenka when they were both away.

Ludmilla had tracked someone down—Gizela Vasa, a young woman living in Ludmilla's own apartment block.

'Gizela sounds ideal,' she enthused. 'She worked for a while at a child-minding crèche, before it had to close.' Ludmilla looked pleased with herself. 'And—if she's suitable, it means you can slowly go back to your work with Pragcine.'

'That is, if Radek still wants me to work with him,' Blažena mused. 'He may have someone else in his sights.'

Ludmilla snorted. 'I doubt that very much. You've already made Pragcine a lot of money, and you're still considered their leading actress.'

'Would this Gizela be willing to come and go as we need her?' Blažena was trying to figure out the logistics of it all. 'Maybe we could ask her to sleep over when we both would be away.'

Ludmilla nodded. 'I'm sure she would do that. After all, she doesn't have any work at the moment. You could make that second bedroom available for her and little Zdenka, if you think it would work.'

'That's a good suggestion.' Blažena smiled. 'Well, can you ask her if she can come for an interview, and we'll take it from there?'

Ludmilla nodded. 'I'll arrange it, and don't worry—once Radek finds out you're here, he'll be on your doorstep, believe me!'

In this, Ludmilla was correct. When Radek learned that Blažena had returned to Prague, he was quick to be in contact and to visit. 'You just take your time. Of course, I want you back with us! And'—here he looked a bit sly— 'if you like, I'll send a copy of the screenplay we were discussing, and you can see how you feel about it.'

Once Blažena had scanned the new screenplay, she felt as if she had never been away from acting. She enthused over it when Radek visited one day.

'You were right—it's perfect for me! It's rather dramatic, but I feel I can really let go with this one. The working title says it all—*Wounded Heart.*' She hesitated. 'Of course, it will be some time before I can leave Zdenka. I don't want to rush things with her.'

Radek was unconcerned. 'Take all the time you want. We have two smaller films to produce during the year, so perhaps early next spring would be a good time to start.'

'Thanks,' Blažena was grateful. 'I should be ready by then.' She gave Radek a shrewd look. 'Just don't find too many glamorous starlets in the meantime!'

Radek put his hand over his heart. 'I promise,' he smiled. 'There can never be another Blažena.' He paused. 'I know I'm changing the subject, but Stefan, our roving cameraman, has just returned from Berlin with more news. You know that they are holding the next Olympic Games in Berlin in August. Well, according to Stefan the German Olympic Committee, with Hitler's blessing, has commissioned Leni Riefenstahl to produce a film about it. She seems to trump Goebbels every time! It will be very interesting to see it.'

'I recall she made *Triumph of the Will*,' Blažena shuddered. 'It was wonderful for its technique, I remember, but terrible for its blatant propaganda.' She sighed. 'I suppose that we can expect the same in the Olympic film. Does film really influence audiences so much?'

Radek shrugged. 'Well, audiences tend to believe what they see on the screen, and especially so if the techniques are superb, and whatever we may think of

Riefenstahl, she is a superb technician as a director and editor.'

* * *

The 1936 Berlin Olympic Games would prove to be controversial for several reasons. Threatened by a boycott of the Games by other nations, Hitler would relent from his rule excluding Jewish and black athletes from competing. German Jewish athletes were to be prevented from taking part.

Ultimately, the Games would prove to be only a partial success for the Nazis. Germany would top the medal tally, but the Americans would triumph in athletics, with the African American Jesse Owens winning four gold medals—an acute embarrassment to his blond, Aryan rivals.

Hitler, for reasons of his own, greeted the German medal winners only, and then left the stadium. When the president of the International Olympic Committee, Henri de Baillet-Latour, remonstrated with Hitler, directing that every medal winner should be congratulated, or none at all, Hitler avoided all further medal ceremonies. Apparently, the Führer was not best pleased that his carefully chosen Aryan athletes were bested by a member of a so-called inferior race.

* * *

Time sped for Blažena. She really felt conflicted. On one hand, she was overjoyed at being a mother and seeing her daughter growing daily. Gizela, with her blazing red hair and fondness for very colourful dresses and chunky necklaces, had proved a natural carer for Zdenka. On the other hand, there was an underlying frustration at not being able to practise her craft. Added to this was the fear that her skills might decline and jeopardise her career. When she voiced her concerns to Radek, he was sympathetic.

'Don't worry—you can keep your skills honed with some coaching. Come up to the Hill occasionally and have some sessions.'

This was such a practical solution that Blažena accepted at once, and for the remainder of the year, she worked from time to time with the company's acting coach. In her spare hours, she read over the screenplay until she was satisfied that she had drawn every nuance from it. She would be back in business once more.

Then, like a whirlwind, Christmas came and the family celebrated the remainder of 1936 back in Rakovník with Miroslav and Helena. Helena looked even more frail but was overjoyed to see little Zdenka, and clucked and cooed over her again.

Early in the new year Blažena, Josef and Zdenka returned to Prague, and all at once another year began, bringing new challenges. The new year should have been joyful, but the news from Rakovník was anything but.

Miroslav rang to say that Helena had died a few months into the year. 'It was peaceful,' he told Blažena, his voice on the line choked with emotion, 'and I know she had been ill for a long time, but I will miss her very much.'

Blažena felt very emotional as well. 'We weren't friends in the beginning, I know,' she admitted, 'but after I left home, we seemed to become much closer. That sounds silly, but it's true. I'll miss her, too. The loveliest thing, though, was that she was able to see Zdenka born, and to know that she had a little step-granddaughter.'

Blažena alone went back for the small funeral, and was shocked at how grief had diminished her father. 'Will you manage here at home?' she asked.

'Oh, yes. I'll stay on here. It's my home, after all. But you must go back to Prague—that's your home, now.'

Blažena returned to Prague with a heavy heart, her sorrow eased by the thought of the reunion with her family. But sorrow rarely travels alone, as she was yet to learn.

CHAPTER TWELVE

Life in Prague went on in almost the same way as before. Josef completed his year-long study course, and was very pleased that this had given him both a salary incrïease and good prospects for tenure. Gizela was proving a gem and was content to remain as official nanny to Zdenka, whom she adored, for the foreseeable future.

Initially, Blažena had been slightly unsure of Gizela when Ludmilla introduced them. With her hair colouring and penchant for bright-coloured dresses and chunky necklaces, Gizela at first had looked too flamboyant to be responsible as a child-carer. But after they had talked with each other and Blažena learnt of Gizela's qualifications, she realised that she truly was fond of children, and had the skills to care for them.

'Why did you have to leave the crèche?' Blažena had been very curious.

Gizela looked downcast. 'The authorities decided that the building was old and unsuitable, and didn't think it worthwhile to find another location. I really miss my little friends.'

Blažena could detect Gizela's sincerity, and the way she was already relating to tiny Zdenka, who was showing great interest in Gizela's necklace.

'I think you would be very suitable for the position,' she had confirmed. 'My husband usually works a standard schedule, but I have a very erratic agenda, and need to be absent at any time. It would mean you would have to be available constantly, and it would be very suitable if you could live in. Is this a problem for you?'

Gizela had smiled broadly. 'That would be a perfect solution. When you're home, perhaps I can assist with other responsibilities. And if I'm lucky, I might be able to sub-lease my apartment, which will help with the money.'

Blažena had related the arrangement to Joseph when he came home. 'Gizela seems to be the perfect solution. Now I feel I could let Radek know that I'm available to start on the next film.' Blažena had the urge to be in action again. 'I'm sure he'll be happy to start on *Wounded Heart.*'

'I don't know about Radek, but I do know you're itching to get back,' Josef said with a smile. 'And why not, if you're confident you can mix motherhood and your career?'

Blažena was excited. 'I'm sure it will work. Gizela is proving to be a wonderful support, and I can organise my life around shoots.'

When she told Radek, he was enthusiastic. 'Great!' he exclaimed. 'We can discuss refining the screenplay, and then start shooting.'

Blažena looked stricken. 'Don't refine it too much—I've spent countless hours studying it. I know it off by heart!'

Radek tempered his enthusiasm slightly. 'I hope that we can continue our business without any problems. By the way, did you know that Mister Hitler's been active again? He's just managed his "Anschluss" by annexing Austria into Germany. After the Austrian Chancellor was assassinated, Hitler threatened to invade Austria, but he didn't have to—the Wehrmacht just waltzed in. 1938 will stand out as a momentous year for Austria.'

Radek's face was grim. 'So, now they have their *Heim ins Reich*—their "Back home to the Empire". It's all about bringing ethnic Germans into the fold. We must remember that Hitler's an Austrian, and has been determined to bring his homeland into Greater Germany.'

Blažena was alarmed. 'I knew Austria had joined Germany, but I had no idea how it was done.'

'It was done the way Hitler usually does things— brutally. And of course, there's still the question of the Sudetenland. If that goes, we'll be the filling in the German sandwich.' Radek threw up his hands in a gesture of futility.

'Will it affect us, and Barrandov's operation?' Blažena was genuinely concerned, not only for herself but also for Radek and all the film-makers in the great studio complex.

'Time will tell, but for the moment, we just keep on producing films, and hope that we can continue.' Radek shrugged. 'It's in the lap of the gods.'

It was as if Blažena had never been away. She slipped effortlessly into the rhythms of film-making, and relished the demands of this more emotionally-demanding role. Previously, her roles were essentially young naïve and innocent women thrust into challenging situations. Now, this role placed her into a slightly older character type—more mature and worldly, and more able to operate from a position of strength.

Maybe they see me as ageing, no longer the one for young roles. Blažena had a momentary frisson of panic. *What if my career is slowly coming to an end?* She gave herself a mental shake. *Nonsense—it just means I am extending my acting powers!* She forced her mind to a more positive perspective, and tried not to worry about the political turmoil growing all around. *I will make this role my best yet. It will be my peak performance as an actress, so that if things go wrong, I will at least have it as my legacy.*

Josef came sauntering into the living room. 'Ah, there you are,' he announced, sitting down and crossing his long legs. 'I'm going away for a few days again.'

'Oh?' Blažena looked up from the screenplay she was scanning. She was keeping one eye on the child, who was on the carpet creating a construction out of coloured blocks, testing each one by biting it before adding it to the pile. 'Where to this time?' She was used to Josef's pilgrimages for opera.

'Ah—Berlin, for this one.' He sounded a little defensive.

'Berlin? At this moment?' Blažena was instantly concerned, remembering her conversation with Radek. 'Do you think it's wise, given all the reports about the increasing Nazi activity there? Vienna's a bit closer, and surely you haven't forgotten that Germany has just annexed Austria in their so-called Anschluss. And what's wrong with our own lovely National Theatre?'

'But this time, it's a very important performance at the *Staatsoper Berlin*—the State Opera House, and they've brought in a talented young conductor— Herbert von Karajan.' Josef tried to sound convincing, reminding Blažena of a little boy determined to get his own way. 'And the Nazis are very pro-culture, you know.'

'Oh?' Blažena looked blank. 'From what they're doing at the moment, you wouldn't think so.'

Josef leant forward, intent on his argument and ignoring Blažena's concern. 'Yes—he's Austrian, but becoming very popular. *His Tristan und Isolde* at the *Staatsoper* made headlines.'

'Oh,' said Blažena again. Over time she had become accustomed to Josef's obsession with opera, but could never warm to it, even given his sometimes-ecstatic descriptions of performances.

'Yes,' Josef's eyes shone with excitement, 'and now he's conducting Richard Strauss's *Rosenkavalier!* It's one of Strauss's most famous operas.'

'Ah, I see,' although Blažena didn't. 'But it's such a long way, don't you think?'

'It's not really—about four to five hours by train, and I can stay overnight.'

Blažena knew from experience that where opera was concerned, Josef was single-minded, and would brook no opposition. Besides, he already would have purchased his opera and train tickets, she was sure.

Acknowledging defeat, she picked up the screenplay. 'When will you go?'

'This Friday,' he replied, 'so I can get the Saturday performance, and then be home on Sunday.'

'So soon?' Blažena was taken aback. 'Well, if you must go, enjoy it, but please travel safely.'

'Don't worry,' Josef bent and kissed her on the forehead. 'I'll be back before you know it!'

Blažena's working week was anything but routine, and she farewelled Josef on Friday. The film industry operated at all hours, and she was busy over the weekend, coming home to the apartment late on Sunday to find Gizela knitting in an armchair and little Zdenka tucked up in bed. There was no sign of Josef.

'No sign of Mister Kozel?' she inquired.

'No, madam,' Gizela shook her head. 'Not even a telephone call.'

Odd—perhaps his train was delayed. With the political situation, schedules could be disrupted. She decided not to worry and prepared herself for bed.

When morning came with still no sign of Josef, Blažena decided to contact Ludmilla to ask Alex if he had any idea of rail disruptions.

'Alex hasn't heard anything about train delays,' Ludmilla could sense that Blažena was becoming concerned. 'Perhaps Radek might know something.'

Blažena determined to ask for Radek's help when she went to the studio. 'It's unusual for him to be late coming home,' she confessed. 'That's why I'm worried.'

Radek looked uneasy. 'It's not the time to be travelling, especially to Berlin,' he muttered. 'You never know what could happen. I suggest we contact the police. I'm quite happy to go with you, if it will help.'

Blažena went with Radek to the police headquarters in central Prague, and outlined her concerns, anxiety etched across her face.

'We will take all the details, but it's very difficult to trace a Czech citizen who has gone out of the country, especially to Germany at a time like this,' shrugged a taciturn official. 'The situation there is very volatile. I suggest you just wait until your husband comes home.'

An increasingly agitated Blažena returned home and struggled to maintain a normal routine in spite of her growing fears. She threw herself into her work during the day, then returned to the apartment to a sympathetic Gizela and a happily gurgling Zdenka—the latter sublimely unaware of the turmoil surrounding her. There, Blažena spent her nights wondering where her husband might be, and hoping against hope that a knock on the door would herald his return.

Days, then weeks passed with no sign of Josef. Then the icy serpent of fear slithered up her spine, as she came to realise that Josef may have disappeared from the face of the earth forever.

CHAPTER THIRTEEN

Blažena's life had turned upside down. Josef's colleagues in the government accounts department were nonplussed, and couldn't shine any light on his disappearance. Sympathetic to her piteous entreaties, Radek went with her several times to the police and passport offices, but they were met with the same results.

'You can take some time away from *Wounded Heart*,' he suggested gently, 'and make more inquiries.'

Blažena looked mutinous. She sat facing him, her hands balled into fists against her thighs. 'No—please! Working on this film is the only thing that's keeping me sane.' She looked directly at him, stress etched across her face. 'And—where would I look, anyway? I don't know anyone in Germany. I would be hopelessly lost. And anyway, as a Czech, I don't dare go into Germany at a time like this.'

'Fine.' Radek knew when he was beaten. 'We'll keep working on the film.'

Blažena threw all her energy into the work, drawing on her grief and tension and injecting them into her character. Radek, her acting colleagues and the crew sometimes just looked on open-mouthed at the depth and fury of her acting. After shooting, sometimes she broke down and wept, but the weeping was cathartic, and although she felt spent, her unhappiness gradually lessened.

Each day, each week, she had fewer tears to shed, and gradually came to an acceptance that it was unlikely she would ever see Josef again.

'I must just carry on,' she confided to Ludmilla one day. 'Life must carry on, if only for Zdenka's sake.'

Ludmilla was sympathetic. 'My darling Blažena, you're young and you're strong. Just look how far you've come—from a shy young girl working in a chemist's shop in a provincial city to a major star in Czech cinema. Believe me, you'll survive, and this, terrible though it is, will make you even stronger.'

Blažena sighed. 'I know, but it will take time. I can survive financially, I know. I've made enough money from films to own our apartment and cope with living expenses.' She looked sombre. 'There's an additional concern—my father is no longer young, and Helena's death has affected him greatly. I'm frightened that he won't ever recover. Miroslav looks older every time I see him.'

It was something that worried Blažena every time she visited her father. Miroslav seemed disconsolate living alone. He had retired, which meant he had even more time to fret alone.

'I know Helena could be a hard woman sometimes,' he confided to Blažena, 'but we loved each other. I thought I would never love another woman after my Ivanka died, but then I met Helena, and I came alive again. But now—' He put his head down, and Blažena could see his tears pooling. She had no way of consoling him, other than to be as supportive as she could. While it was difficult, it was at least a distraction from her own problems, which surfaced when she had to return to Prague.

There, she took to walking occasionally in the evening along the embankment towards Charles Bridge to ease her emotional turmoil, her gaze unseeing on its gentle arch with the medieval gates at either end. River mist wrapped around the vast stone piers like a ghost lover. Beyond, Hradčany rose, with the spires of St Vitus Cathedral piercing a dark sky smudged with cloud.

She wandered under the linden trees, hands thrust deep into her coat pockets, her shoes scattering the carpet of fallen russet leaves. The Vltava flowed gently beside her, but she was deaf to its murmurings.

She went along the embankment to where the river's famous swans, some of them paired as mates, glided elegantly around the stone piers. She went as far as the approach to the bridge and stared up at the statue of Charles IV, which seemed in her mind to gaze down at her benevolently. She could not bring herself to walk onto the bridge itself, because the memory of the evening when Josef proposed to her and she accepted was unbearable. *How could this happen?* The bile of her grief rose up her throat. *Could you live with someone for years and really know them? Know everything about them? Nothing about them?* Her mind seethed with questions, but no answers came.

* * *

'Stefan! How did it go in Germany? Did you have any issues getting in or out?' Radek had not seen the popular cameraman since he left for Germany to see a screening of Leni Riefenstahl's film celebrating the 1936 Olympic Games. It wasn't until April 1938 that it had its cinema release.

'Fine!' Stefan was enthusiastic, and only wanted to talk about the film. 'Riefenstahl used so many technical effects that it was dazzling. She made it in two parts. The first was *Festival of the Nations*, and the second was *Festival of Beauty*. One outstanding technique was her camera setup for the diving in the second part. Absolutely stunning! One minute the diver's in the air, the next you see him underwater. It became pure aquatic ballet.'

Stefan shrugged. 'It's perfection in film-making—and also perfect propaganda. You have to admire her technique, though.' He paused. 'Riefenstahl even included Jesse Owens' track and field victories, and as an African American, he was the complete opposite of a perfect Aryan! What a disappointment to Herr Hitler. Whatever, you must see it!'

'Did you have any problems going there and coming back?' Radek was concerned for Stefan but also had Blažena and her crisis in mind.

Stefan shrugged. 'No, not really. There's more police and military presence, but I do have some colleagues there who work in film, and they made things easier. Whatever, you can sense change in the air—and it's not a nice smell!'

* * *

Then came a situation that had everyone on edge— one that forced Blažena's personal dilemma into the background. Alex and Ludmilla were trying to make sense of what was happening as they met in Blažena's apartment one evening in late September. Blažena and Gizela had prepared *chlebiček*, the delicious Czech snack of baguette slices topped with different meats, potato salad, cheese and mayonnaise. Normally, they would be consumed with great pleasure, but this time they sat abandoned on the table. No-one had an appetite, and the atmosphere was subdued.

What everyone had feared had actually happened. Germany had annexed the Sudetenland. In March, Hitler had made himself the advocate for the German-speaking people in the Sudetenland areas, inciting unrest between them and their Czech neighbours.

Blažena was bewildered. 'There was to be a meeting in Munich this month, to agree on a solution, wasn't there?'

Alex was, uncharacteristically for him, white-hot with anger. 'They had a meeting in Munich all right, but guess what—Germany, France and England were invited, but not Czechoslovakia!'

'That can't be right—surely it couldn't happen like that!' Blažena was incredulous.

'That's exactly how it happened.' Alex was positive. He ran his fingers through his hair in frustration. 'Hitler for Germany, Didier for France and Chamberlain for England were there, and nobody from our government! And'—he threw his hands up in disgust—'it was engineered by Hermann Göring, using Italy's Benito Mussolini as his mouthpiece!'

'What happened after that?' Ludmilla was trying to understand the implications of it all.

'After that?' Alex exploded. 'The Germans just walked into the Sudetenland! This is exactly what they wanted all along. Now, we're almost surrounded! They call it the Munich Agreement, but we should call it the Munich Betrayal!'

There was silence. 'Radek will be on tenterhooks,' Blažena murmured after a while. 'He anticipated something like this a few years ago, and he was right. It may have consequences for our film industry.'

She was correct. Radek looked tired, as though he had not been sleeping well. 'Things are going from bad to worse,' he muttered to her in the Barrandov studio office one day, 'and I can't see a way out of it. Luckily, most of the work on *Wounded Heart* is done. The shooting is finished, and we're now on to post-production. It should be ready for release just before Christmas. We hope it will be a success. It's a strong story, and it has your name as the lead.' He smiled as a nostalgic thought occurred to him. 'Do you remember how we tried to find a screen name for you in your early days?'

Blažena smiled in return. 'Yes—I couldn't think of anything except my first name, and so I became "Blažena". It seems to have stuck.'

Radek nodded. 'Well, it's worked really well for you, just like a single name is working for the Swedish actress Greta Garbo. She's internationally famous, and just known as "Garbo", so—congratulations!' He made a tiny bow.

Blažena managed a smile at that, remembering their very first encounter. Then she just had to laugh. 'That's what got me into this in the first place! We really have made a great team, haven't we?'

'Yes.' Radek looked serious. 'It's been a long time now, and we both have changed—and been changed by circumstance, and maybe simply fate. I wonder just what's in store for us in the new year?'

'Maybe it's best not to think too much about that,' Blažena ventured, 'otherwise, we might not have the strength to carry on. Let's just take things as they come.'

She was feeling somewhat fatalistic. The year had been an extremely difficult one, and recent events had cast a pall of gloom over everyone. Blažena fingered her gold locket. *What will the new year bring?*

CHAPTER FOURTEEN

The new year only brought a heavy sense of unease. Disturbing rumours flew around like ravens. The contradictory gossip only served to instil a sense of apathy in people. For Blažena, the indecision was caused by more specific reasons. There was uncertainty at Pragcine as to whether they should consider starting on a new project or not.

Since *Wounded Heart* was finished, she had taken the opportunity to visit her father again. The cold winter had taken its toll on Miroslav, who now looked very frail.

Blažena was concerned. 'Why don't you come to Prague with me and stay a while in the apartment?'

'My home is here, my darling girl.' Miroslav looked around him—the comfortable chair with colourful cushions, and a standard reading light beside a table placed within easy reach. 'This is my home, and here I want to stay.' He raised a hand to counter any argument. 'My neighbours are kind and drop in to see me, and often they bring some food so I don't starve. Do you remember Tereza Beranková? She visits regularly.' He shrugged his shoulders. 'So, you see, I'm coping well enough.'

Blažena noticed a walking stick, half concealed by the chair's arm, but knew well enough not to argue. She could sense the same kind of stubbornness that she felt in herself, and she returned to Prague feeling frustrated at having achieved nothing. In early March, she made the trip to Barrandov to see Radek but found that Pragcine, like the other independent studios, was caught up in the same inertia, unwilling to commit to new projects.

'Do you think the situation is so bad?' Blažena was always eager to take on the challenge of a new film. 'Why is no-one making a move?'

Radek looked even more haggard, his face etched with lines and his once light brown hair now sprinkled with grey. 'We've been hearing that the government is having problems again with Germany. Our Prime Minister Emil Hácha is very weak. Some even say he's senile, but we know he's frightened of Hungary. There is talk that he might even try to do a deal with Hitler, whatever that might involve.'

Blažena gasped. 'But that would be disastrous! It would be like the sheep making a deal with the wolf!'

Radek shrugged. 'Who can say? But it means that our future is very uncertain. It could be very risky for us to embark on a new project.'

Radek had been more prophetic than he realised. Because of his fear of Hungary, Hácha begged the German Wehrmacht for protection and Hitler agreed to form a protectorate, but then played his winning hand—he threatened to bomb Prague unless the Czechs allowed free passage for German troops to enter the country. The feeble Hácha yielded, and on the fifteenth of March, Germany took Czechoslovakia. Ironically, Adolf Hitler made his first and last visit to Prague.

On the Saturday after occupation, life seemed relatively normal. Blažena and Radek, who had come from the city Pragcine office, were waiting in Kavarna Slavia for a session with Ludmilla and Alex. The café had become a comfort zone, with its elegant fittings and its piano softly playing in the background.

'I hope they're all right,' Blažena murmured. 'They're coming from Ludmilla's apartment, and it's not too far away.'

Radek was reassuring. 'Probably they're just being careful. The Germans are still driving around.'

* * *

Alex and Ludmilla were preparing to leave their apartment. Both had wisely donned coats, scarves and gloves to combat the cold in the streets outside.

'Have we got everything?' Ludmilla was a stickler for detail, including all-important keys.

Alex, winding his scarf around his neck, grinned. 'Yes—all present and correct.'

They stepped out into the street, and made their way towards Narodní and Kavarna Slavia. They walked arm in arm along Bartolomějská Street and were turning into a side street, when two German staff cars tore around the corner just as they were leaving the narrow footpath.

Ludmilla shrieked. Alex shouted, 'Careful!' as he pulled Ludmilla back onto the footpath, narrowly avoiding the vehicles. The drivers and occupants of the vehicles shouted something in guttural German and sped off.

'Are you all right?' asked Alex anxiously.

'I—I think so.' Ludmilla was shaking. 'But why did they have to drive so recklessly? They could have killed us!'

'They're behaving as if they own the place!' Alex fumed. 'Well, maybe they do, now!'

They burst through the doors of Kavarna Slavia, their breath still misting from the chilly outside air.

'Oh, that's better!' Alex removed his gloves and rubbed his hands together.

'We were becoming worried,' Blažena said. 'We hoped there hadn't been any trouble.'

Alex and Ludmilla took their seats and ordered coffee. 'Well,' Alex said, frowning, 'not exactly trouble, but Germans are driving everywhere, and don't care if people are trying to cross the roads. We had to move quickly once or twice.' His expression was grim. 'We almost got hit by a couple of their vehicles.'

They recounted their experience in detail, to the alarm of Blažena and Radek.

'I think you need a shot of *slivovice* to get over that,' observed Radek. 'In fact, I think we all need one!'

He ordered the drinks and they settled down to try to make sense of their changed circumstances.

'To think just last Wednesday the Germans came in through a blinding snowstorm and some of their vehicles broke down, but that didn't stop them,' Blažena recalled, 'and some people on the roads even threw snowballs!' She sighed. 'What a pathetic thing to do, and yet how brave.'

Ludmilla was despondent. 'I saw their dreadful trucks and cars along Národní Street,' She shuddered. 'The staff cars with officers had those swastika pennants, and big troop carriers had a large German cross on the sides. I'm frightened we won't be safe in our beds.' She thought of those vehicles, with the soldiers stony-faced and menacing, lumbering along the beautiful street, the steel treads grinding on the historic cobblestones. 'And the worst thing is, some of our people even were waving small swastika flags as they went by. How could they!' Ludmilla's expression was furious.

There was silence as everyone stared at her. For Ludmilla to be so upset was a rarity.

She looked at them all in turn, then looked at Alex apologetically. 'I was there, but I didn't tell you.' She spoke softly, forcing herself to a memory she would rather erase.

Ludmilla choked back a sob. 'I was given a task by my department to take some documents up to Hradčany.' She paused and drew a deep breath. 'When I came out, there were soldiers lined up near one of the entrances. Other people were there, too, maybe just curious about what might be happening. The soldiers all looked up at one of the windows, and the people did, as well. The soldiers were giving the Nazi salute, and some of the crowd were, too.'

Ludmilla's eyes were stricken. 'I looked up, and there he was, looking out on Prague from the window. There was no mistaking that lank hair combed across the forehead and that postage stamp of a moustache. It was that dreadful creature, Hitler. He must just have come into the city.' She drew a shuddering breath. 'He was standing there as if he was lord of all he surveyed, which I suppose he was.' Ludmilla's tone was bitter, her voice almost failing her, and she could hardly speak for her grief and anger. 'And the next day, he turned us into a Nazi Protectorate!'

Radek broke the silence that followed. 'I heard that Czechs were giving the Germans the wrong directions, if it's any consolation.' He smiled grimly. 'But no doubt they will get to where they want, eventually. Hitler certainly did.' He shrugged. 'The more people oppose the Germans, the more angry it will make them. Just think about all those people who went to Wenceslas Square and sang the National Anthem—that's like kicking a hornet's nest.' He ordered a shot of *slivovice* from a passing waiter and downed it immediately when it arrived. 'Ah—I needed that!'

'But that's just being patriotic,' Blažena cut in, 'like when someone placed a photograph of our first president, Masaryk, on the Tomb of the Unknown Soldier! The Germans must expect some reaction, surely, and they wouldn't be so brutal as to react aggressively to it.'

Alex, unusually quiet, toyed with his cake, but looked up. 'It was a betrayal of the Munich Pact,' he murmured. 'Hácha just folded, and now we're under German control. And we know why they were so eager to take us over—we have a strong industry base, and also good military production facilities. It's a means to an end!' He seemed resigned.

Blažena and Ludmilla looked at each other in surprise. Lately, Alex had become a hothead. Blažena had felt uneasy for him, as vocal opposition to a changing political system could have dangerous consequences. She was glad that he seemed to be a bit calmer, and had not totally become a political animal, for Ludmilla's sake as well as his own. Being outspoken and overheard could now be very dangerous for anyone.

She made an attempt at restoring everyone's confidence. 'Changes will come, but they could just be minor, and maybe we could get on with our lives.' Even as she spoke, she felt that she was uttering a falsehood for, to all of them, it was obvious that changes would not be minor but threatening to tear down the very fabric of their society.

It was self-delusion, she admitted to herself—only an attempt to be positive and say something to dispel the gloom surrounding them. Privately, she was uneasy, wondering whether she and her child would be safe. With a sharp pang in her heart, she wondered where Josef might be, and if he was still alive and safe, too.

Now she understood the concern Radek had felt over time. He, of all of them, had the most to lose. She knew Radek to be level-headed and diplomatic. He, if anyone, should be able to weather this brewing storm.

Things would change, Blažena knew, but privately doubted that they would be for the better. Again, her thoughts went to Josef. *Surely, he couldn't be involved in any subversive activity—he was always so satisfied with his accounting career.* She wondered if his easy-going nature was just a façade. *Was his obsession with opera what it appeared, or was there some underlying motive for his frequent absences? Did I really ever know my handsome Josef?* These disturbing thoughts swarmed around in her mind like wasps. She strove to lighten her mood and focus on her friends. *Whatever happens, I owe my loyalty to Radek.* She was determined. *He is the reason for my success, and he's my strongest ally.*

When everyone else had left, Blažena sat in the café while the shadows gathered outside, considering her future and that of those whom she loved. An occasional occupying army vehicle rolled by—a reminder of the catastrophe that had befallen them. Radek's happiness was important to her, and she made the decision to bring up the subject of starting a new project, if only as a distraction for him—and for herself.

CHAPTER FIFTEEN

The trams appeared to be operating as usual, so Blažena took the opportunity to see Radek. As her tram rattled its way up to the plateau the following day, she couldn't help smiling at the familiarity of it, and she reflected on how much she loved Prague and the career she had been granted. Surely this beautiful place would survive, even in these difficult circumstances. *I must persuade Radek to start something—anything*. She believed the time for inertia was past, and she needed to meet Radek face-to-face.

'Why do you want us to start a project? We have no idea how we are situated now that Germany has invaded us.' In the Pragcine studio office Radek folded his arms on his desk, his expression neutral. Blažena was eager, her eyes sparkling.

Blažena defended her suggestion. 'Because I think it's better to do something rather than to do nothing, and because it means everyone retains their professional skills if they're occupied.' She warmed to her theme. 'Perhaps you could consider something lighter in nature rather than a drama.'

'You mean a comedy?' Radek's face went slack with shock. 'In these uncertain times?'

'Maybe that's just what people would appreciate now—what better than to give them something to take their minds off their worries?'

Radek was weakening, she could tell. 'Let me think about it,' he said, 'and I'll consult the others in the production team.' He sighed. 'You know how nervous everyone is these days. I'll have to be very diplomatic.' Blažena heaved a sigh of relief. At least she had planted a seed, and maybe something might grow from it.

During the following months, the effects of the German invasion began to show. Some people committed suicide in despair at the loss of their country's independence. Everyone had to obtain new identification papers.

'So how do we do that?' Blažena was talking to Ludmilla, who had heard of the new requirement.

Ludmilla shrugged. 'I suppose we have to go to the City Hall. No doubt someone will tell us what to do. But—for some reason, we all have to produce a family tree going back to our grandparents' era to prove that we're Czech. Some people are going to find that a bit difficult, and I hate to think what will happen to them if they can't.'

Blažena wondered at this. 'That seems an odd requirement. Why do they need that?'

Ludmilla sighed. 'Well, apparently we all have to state that we're neither Jewish nor Romany.'

'Why is that so important?' Blažena asked Ludmilla. 'Aren't we all Czech?'

Ludmilla was disgusted. 'Apparently, the Germans regard Jews and Romanies as members of inferior races,' she explained. 'They don't fall into the accepted category of being pure Aryan. We Czechs have the potential to become "Aryanised"—made acceptable to Nazi eyes.'

'But no Czechs are pure Aryan, surely,' Blažena protested. 'We're predominantly Slavic, aren't we?' She couldn't see what difference it made. 'Aren't we all just people?'

'In a perfect world or maybe in one of your romantic films, possibly,' Ludmilla muttered, 'but I have a very bad feeling about the future for those people being singled out. The Nazis have this obsession with racial purity, and no-one will escape it.'

* * *

As time passed, more evidence of Nazi occupation made itself obvious, like a steel band slowly forcing a stranglehold on the Czech way of life. Shop owners who could prove they were truly Czech were permitted to remain open. Other shops, presumably Jewish, were closed and boarded up. No-one dared speak of their owners, who simply disappeared. Worse, sometimes the boarded-up shops reopened under new management, a clear indication that their previous owners had been betrayed to the invader.

Gizela came home to the apartment one day quite agitated. She had been out looking for books suitable for Zdenka. 'Do you know, they are removing a lot of Czech books—books about our history, our culture and language, and now there are a lot of books about German life and culture.'

'That's monstrous,' said Blažena. 'What harm can our books do?'

'Nothing, I would have thought,' said Gizela almost tearfully, 'and the word around is that they are replacing some of the upper school textbooks with books favouring Nazism. Our children are going to be brainwashed!' She drew a shuddering breath. 'Everything is being taken from us. We're having periodic blackouts, so some people took advantage to paint large "V" letters on buildings, just to show our resistance. Now, the Germans have taken it for their own, and it's everywhere! It's just another example of their horrible propaganda!'

Blažena nodded in sympathy, recalling the increasing number of crimson Nazi banners with their odious swastikas bleeding down the walls of public buildings. 'I know how you feel,' she murmured, 'but if you think this is bad, I think it's going to get a lot worse.'

Gizela fingered her chunky necklace nervously. She understood only too well. Several times she had observed SS guards in their intimidating black uniforms, stalking the streets like crows seeking prey. People trying to shop avoided big intersections, preferring side streets and lanes and then scurrying home, heads down. Fear ruled the streets, and the atmosphere was like a pall of darkness smothering the city.

Blažena tried to contact Radek several times but often the telephone system was intermittent or he was unable to answer. Eventually, she tried the Pragcine city office and went to see him. He looked very stressed, shuffling papers on his desk in an aimless way.

'I've had one or two visits from men in black uniforms who are interested in the Barrandov operation. I have the feeling that we will be changed, and not through our own choice. Obviously, everything depends on Goebbels. He thinks film production here is potentially safer than at Babelsberg in Germany.'

Blažena picked up on his meaning. 'What will it mean?'

'I'm not sure. Time will tell,' Radek murmured. 'Goebbels may have a soft spot for Havel.'

'Why on earth would he?' Blažena was confused.

'Well,' Radek explained, 'Havel was behind promoting Baarová in making some of her best films, and we know the relationship there.' He shrugged. 'We won't start any new project yet, just in case.'

* * *

Radek was wiser than he thought. One day, not long after his conversation with Blažena, a staff car bearing the squared German cross on the sides pulled up outside the reception entrance near Barrandov's impressive central tower. Secretaries peered out curiously at this strange sight. An officer in a grey adjutant's uniform strode to the desk.

'Who is in charge here?' he barked.

The flustered receptionist was out of her depth. 'There are several independent studios here, but Mr Miloš Havel is in charge of Barrandov Studios overall.'

The adjutant looked down an aquiline nose. 'Have everyone assembled here in half an hour.' With that, he raised his right arm in a salute. '*Heil Hitler!*' He turned on his heel, strode back to the car and drove off.

In a panic, the secretary did his bidding, and presently everyone grouped in the reception area, wondering what was happening.

Another car arrived. No ordinary vehicle, this was a large black Mercedes-Benz 770 bearing swastika pennants. An adjutant leapt out and opened the rear door, standing to attention. A short man wearing a hat and long coat emerged, and walked with a slight limp into the reception.

Several people gasped in shock, recognising the deep-set eyes and straight slit of a mouth. It was Joseph Goebbels, the Reich Minister of Propaganda. His hooded eyes raked the group, seeking out Miloš Havel.

'*Herr Havel*,' he grated, 'these studios are hereby confiscated by the German Reich. You will be informed of any further actions at a later date. *Heil Hitler*!' He gave the arrogant Nazi salute, turned and limped back to his waiting car. In the reception area, Miloš Havel was ashen-faced and almost fainted from shock. His secretary helped him to a chair where he sat, trying to comprehend what had just happened. Cinema was the love of his life. He had poured large amounts of money into the development of the industry and he had given all his energy to it. Now it looked like it was all going to be snatched away.

* * *

Things moved swiftly. Miloš Havel was forced to sell his share in Barrandov Studios, but permitted to remain in charge. The original AB Corporation was replaced by Deutsche Prag-Film. The only saving grace was that all staff were protected from persecution, and could continue working. Apparently, Goebbels' reasoning was that for an efficient transfer to making propaganda films, knowledgeable staff were an essential element.

Blažena was encouraging. 'That must be a good thing, surely. Possibly it just means the change of name, and we could operate as usual. Maybe we could do that lighter film—the Nazis couldn't object to that, could they?'

Radek looked up tiredly from his desk in the office where they were discussing this shocking new development. 'Goebbels will just eat us,' he murmured softly. 'After all, he's Hitler's Minister for Propaganda, and a very powerful man.'

Blažena tried to be more positive. 'Surely, he will see that Barrandov is an efficient, well-run organisation. Maybe things will go smoothly from now on.'

'I hope you're right,' Radek muttered, 'but I wouldn't hold my breath.'

Blažena could not have been more wrong. Western Europe's reluctance to curb Hitler's aggressive actions was to prove disastrous. On the first of September 1939, Hitler's forces invaded Poland. Britain held to its promise of action along with its ally France. Hitler's strength was boosted by his then-allies, the Soviet Union and the Slovak Republic, and the world would never be the same again.

CHAPTER SIXTEEN

A perception of disbelief circulated. Some, like Radek, Blažena and her friends and associates, had hoped against hope that it wouldn't come to this. But now, the brutal truth descended like a hammer blow—Czechoslovakia was at war, albeit reluctantly, with a growing number of European countries. Because Hitler failed to withdraw his troops from Poland, England's Prime Minister Neville Chamberlain, supported by France, had declared war on Germany two days later, and the die was cast.

Radek was desolate, as were the other directors operating at Barrandov Studios. Goebbels' agents warned that, unless they submitted to Nazi ideology, they would be forced into so-called internal emigration—in other words, prevented from working.

'I don't know what to do,' Radek confided to Blažena. 'Maybe we could continue, even at the loss of our independence.' He sighed in frustration. 'It's the only thing that might help us survive. Of course, they will censor everything we do, and all films must have German subtitles.'

'But at least you can continue to make films, even given the strictures they impose. It's better than doing nothing. So, why not submit a light film, as I suggested—not necessarily a comedy, but something non-threatening, that would show a willingness to cooperate.'

Radek smiled. 'You've had that in your head all along, haven't you?' He gave her a straight look. 'They have had their eye on you, so I hear. Apparently, your fame has travelled far and wide.'

'Me?' Blažena was shocked. 'Why me?' She was alarmed that she had come under the gaze of the Reich.

'Well, you do look the perfect Aryan, with your eye and hair colour!' Radek smiled grimly. 'That could have a lot to do with it. If we could produce another film starring you, it would smooth our way somewhat.'

Blažena had mixed feelings. It would mean she could delve into work again, but on the other hand, she felt she was being used as a pawn in Goebbels' propaganda machine. She sighed. She knew she owed a great deal to Radek, and felt this was the time to show her gratitude.

'Very well,' she conceded, 'If it means we can continue to work, I'll do it.'

* * *

Work on *A Country Girl* started soon, after being approved by the Nazi censors. It paved the way for Radek and the former Pragcine staff to continue working, although Barrandov was being swamped by German crews making both German-language and Czech-language films.

'There's talk that Goebbels is going to construct three new sound stages,' Radek confided one day. 'Apparently he's concerned that the film production studios at Babelsberg near Berlin might be in danger from future Allied air raids.'

'That could be a good thing, couldn't it?' Blažena considered. 'That could mean the potential for more productions here.' She was happy that the company could start on a new production, even under the vigilant Nazi eye. It meant a possible future for them all.

As shooting on *A Country Girl* progressed, Blažena was relaxing between scenes in the sound studio one day, reviewing her script. She became aware of a lull in activity and voices, and turned around in her chair.

'*Ja*, perfect Aryan womanhood! A very good choice!' Goebbels stood there, in front of a group of uniformed officers. His deep-set eyes had dark shadows under them, but he stared at Blažena with a reptilian intensity that made her nervous. He was in uniform, holding his cap. Blažena couldn't help staring at his high hairline. When he spoke, the words came like those of a ventriloquist out of his thin-lipped mouth.

He bowed stiffly. '*Fräulein Blažena*,' he rasped, 'I wish you all success in this film for the Reich.'

'Th—thank you, *Herr Goebbels*,' Blažena stuttered, reluctant to betray her shock by saying anything more.

Goebbels nodded, turned on his heel and limped away. Blažena remained seated, shaken by the encounter.

* * *

'It was his eyes that were so frightening,' she related to Gizela that evening. 'They just seemed to look right through me, and they were so cold. Chilling.' She shuddered. 'I'm not going to forget them for a very long time. And, I feel repulsed by his approval. I feel besmirched!' She continued to study her screenplay when Gizela took a telephone call. She called Blažena to the instrument. Blažena picked up the receiver to hear muffled sobbing. 'Hello,' she said, 'who is it?'

'Dear Blažena.' A woman was struggling to speak. 'It's Beranková—Tereza Beranková speaking. I'm a neighbour of Mister Kalin's. I'm terribly sorry, but'— here the caller burst into tears again—'Mister Kalin died a short while ago. We were having supper at our house, when your dear father choked and collapsed. I called the doctor, but he was gone.'

Blažena stood like a statue. Grief immobilised her, and she could barely continue the conversation, assuring Mrs Beranková that she would do everything necessary. Then she collapsed in tears, Gizela trying to console her. Zdenka, sensing the distraught mood, started to cry as well, and it was some time before calm ensued. When Blažena had calmed a little, she realised that, apart from her overwhelming grief, the final link to her family and her childhood had been severed.

* * *

'Of course you must go,' Radek was adamant. 'Take what time you need.'

Blažena was grateful. 'Thank you—it will only be me and a few of my father's friends and neighbours at the funeral. I'll be back soon.'

Blažena's journey to Rakovník was marred this time by German checkpoints, where officious Nazi soldiers checked everyone's papers. It made for a long and stressful trip, given what was ahead.

Eventually the ordeal was over—her father buried and the house cleared—and she could leave for the return journey. She leant against the bus window and stared unseeing at the passing countryside. She fingered her precious locket. *First my mother, then Helena, and now my father. And what of Josef? I may never know.* She sighed. *I only know I'm now alone in the world.*

In time the house would become hers, but she couldn't contemplate living in it within the foreseeable future. Prague would have to be her base while she was still able to work. What might come after was still a blank page.

As time passed, the vice of the German occupiers tightened even further. Apart from the regular SS searches, more and more Jewish-owned shops closed and their owners disappeared. It was not generally known that many Jewish people from Prague and the Sudetenland were shipped to Terezín, a town north of Prague. Word was that the Gestapo were assigned to create a model ghetto and concentration camp there.

***

Prague had always been a rich city, with well-stocked stores and a wide range of luxury goods. With the invasion, the situation changed dramatically.

'What do you mean, you have nothing?' Blažena was shopping for children's wear.

'I'm sorry, but we can't get stock in,' the saleswoman said with a shrug. 'There is nothing to be had.'

'We'll just have to make do,' Gizela said later, when Blažena had recounted her frustrated shopping excursion. 'I can sew. We'll have to let out seams and alter, that's all.'

'There will be a lot of altering in the studio costume departments,' Blažena mused. 'No more nice new costumes for the time being, I'll guarantee!'

* * *

Because civic offices were in a state of confusion and workers were reluctant to be seen by vigilant Nazi patrols, the city began to look run-down. Rubbish accumulated in the streets. More people took to getting around by bicycle, as the use of private cars was increasingly discouraged. Nazi law forced the remaining drivers to use the right-hand side.

Kavarna Slavia continued to act as their refuge from the deteriorating conditions, although there were fewer staff and patrons, and there was always the risk of a German uniform or leather-coated Gestapo lurking, eavesdropping.

Alex was despondent. 'Things are difficult at work,' he confided. 'There is always someone snooping around, checking everything that we need to print. A lot gets censored, and that's really bad for our business. Plus, now we have to print some of their propaganda as well.' He grimaced as though he had a bad taste in his mouth.

'Everyone is uneasy about the Germans.' Radek had been keeping his ears open to gossip. 'There are rumours that people are fighting back.' He looked around. 'Apparently, resistance groups are forming. There are reports of sabotage of German vehicles and checkpoints. Some working groups are preparing to strike.'

Ludmilla looked concerned. 'That's all very well,' she considered, 'but don't you think that these actions will provoke the Nazis? They won't take them lying down.'

They looked at her and then at each other. What she had said made sense, and knowing the vicious nature of their occupiers, reprisals were not only possible but inevitable.

* * *

It was no coincidence that the Nazi hierarchy was considering just that. In his Berlin office, The Führer was haranguing two members of his inner circle that their occupation strictures were not working. The softer approach to dealing with the Czech people was leading to a sense of rebellion. Strikes were increasing and sabotage was proving an obstacle to military production. Hitler was furious. 'We must bring the Czech vermin into line!' he snarled.

Heinrich Himmler, a leading member of the Nazi Party and one of the most powerful men in Germany, looked up expectantly, but Hitler cast his gaze to the third man—a tall, slim high-ranking German SS and police official. The Führer stabbed a finger at him. 'I make you responsible for this!'

The third man nodded his acceptance. His name was Reinhard Heydrich. His policies, and the events which would succeed them, would unleash a reign of terror that would resonate down through time.

CHAPTER SEVENTEEN

Reinhard Tristan Eugen Heydrich would prove to be somewhat of a contradiction.

'The man has become a monster,' Alex was talking with Ludmilla in her apartment. Being private was the only way to have a conversation these days, given the presence of Gestapo and SS personnel everywhere. 'And,' he continued, 'it's a bit strange, given his background.'

Ludmilla was both fascinated and repelled by the man. 'Why is that?' she asked.

'Well, he was born into a family with high social standing. Reinhard himself was even an altar boy, given that his mother was Catholic. His father was a composer and opera singer, and his mother was a talented pianist. In fact, his father founded a conservatory of music and drama, the Halle Conservatory of Music, Theatre, and Teaching, and his mother taught there. Heydrich himself even has operatic names—Reinhard after an opera written by his father, and Tristan after Richard Wagner's *Tristan und Isolde*.'

Ludmilla snorted. 'That's odd, considering how he turned out.'

'There could be a reason for that,' Alex said. 'Apparently, as a student, he was frequently bullied because he had a high-pitched voice, and always had issues with accusations that he was Jewish. There was this contradiction about him—on one side he was very academic and artistic, and on the other, he was an accomplished athlete. Rumour has it that he was very frail as a child, and his parents encouraged him strongly into physical activity.'

'And was he Jewish?' Ludmilla asked.

'No,' Alex replied, 'but it took an investigation to prove that he wasn't, and maybe that stigma fuelled his hatred of Jewish people. Something certainly did.'

'Well, it didn't prevent him from gaining a lot of power,' Ludmilla muttered.

Alex grimaced. 'You're right. Even though there were scandals about his womanising, and being thrown out of the German Navy, he's ended up virtually as the dictator of Bohemia and Moravia. Maybe he just had a determination to gain power and influence. And now'—Alex's face hardened— 'he's been given authority to implement a "final solution" to the so-called Jewish question.'

Ludmilla looked horrified. 'What does that really mean?'

'If it means what people fear it means, it's the extermination of the Jews in those countries under German control.'

* * *

Heydrich was appointed Deputy Reich Protector in the autumn of 1941 and wasted no time in making himself one of the most hated men in Czechoslovakia. He declared martial law, and began a reign of terror calculated to bring Czechs into line. His first victims were resistance fighters already under arrest and imprisoned.

At work, Alex was concentrating as he was designing a lithograph plate for a book illustration—a precision task which took great care. One careless move in the execution of the image, and all would be ruined.

'Stop what you are doing!' A gruff voice in his ear made him look up abruptly. A Gestapo agent was standing next to him. He produced grim photographs. 'You are to make posters of these traitors to the Reich. They have all been executed. Here is the text. You have twenty-four hours.'

Horrified, Alex sought his manager's eye, but his superior nodded imperceptibly. There was no option but to obey. Alex reluctantly took the horrifying images in the photographs and went about transferring them.

* * *

'I don't know how long I can do this!' Alex sat with his head in his hands in their apartment kitchen that evening.

Ludmilla looked up from making coffee and put her hand on his shoulder. 'What's so terrible?' she asked.

'Not only do we have to work with the Gestapo breathing down our necks at the printing business, but now we have to produce posters of all the people Heydrich has had executed, so they can be displayed all over Prague!'

'That's terrible!' Ludmilla sat down at the table. 'You do know that he's being called the "Butcher of Prague"?'

Alex groaned. 'Yes—and he's very quickly earning that title. The man is a monster, and Heaven help us all with him in charge. He's determined to reverse the so-called soft approach to controlling us, and he's taking it to extreme. His aim is to "Germanise" us, whatever that means. I don't think I want to know! Hitler is so impressed that he calls him "the man with the iron heart", and regards that as a compliment! He swans around in that huge open car of his as though he were some kind of god.'

'Maybe he's so sure of what he's doing that he thinks he's untouchable.' Ludmilla considered a moment. 'The thing is, I hear he's apparently having some good results in spite of his terror tactics.'

'What could be good, coming from him?' Alex stared at her in disbelief.

'I don't know if it's true,' Ludmilla murmured, 'but I've heard that Prague is going to be cleaned up, even if it takes prison labour, and apparently gymnastic events are going to be organised for workers, to improve morale.'

Alex sneered. 'Well, the workers are very important—they're vital for the production of military equipment for the Reich!'

'Well,' Ludmilla sighed, 'if our living conditions improve even a little, it's good.'

* * *

Under Heydrich's rule, life became more normal, and during the remainder of the year living conditions actually improved, but at the expense of longer, harder working hours. Heydrich even raised pensions. Even though a Nazi, he was an educated man, and he organised cultural events like orchestral concerts. These were held mostly in the famous Rudolfinum and featured the German Philharmonic Orchestra.

'Just more propaganda,' Radek muttered when he saw the concert posters going up.

Other examples followed. Facing the Rudolfinum, Smetana Square, named in honour of the father of

Czech music, was renamed *Mozartplatz*—Mozart Square.

'That's appalling!' Blažena exclaimed when Radek told her of the change.

'There's more to it,' Radek chuckled. 'Rumour has it, Heydrich wanted the statue of Felix Mendelssohn, who was Jewish, removed from the Rudolfinum's roof, but when they got up there, they didn't know one from the other, so they accidentally took Wagner's statue down!' Blažena just stared. 'But,' Radek laughed, 'Wagner never was there, so it's anybody's guess who they removed! It's a good story, anyway.'

This was, of course, all part of Heydrich's Germanisation of the Czechs, and his ultimate aim was to bring suitable candidates into the greater German realm, while unsuitable members of the populace were destined for either reallocation or extermination.

Blažena was not affected by the rigours of the general régime, since Goebbels had absorbed all of Barrandov's operations into his Deutsche Prag-Film, and was busily creating films in German and Czech. Luckily, *A Country Girl* was proceeding well, which meant Blažena and Radek both had work, although Radek still mourned the loss of his own production company Pragcine.

Removing her make-up after a shoot one day, Blažena turned to find Radek in her dressing room.

'How are you finding the situation now?' Radek asked. 'Does the constant censorship bother you?'

'No, not really. It's a bit like a straitjacket, but if we play by the rules, we might survive.' Blažena smiled wryly. 'Life's a bit like living inside a film itself nowadays. Let's just hope we have a happy ending. There is one problem, though.'

'What's that?' Radek was concerned.

'Well,' Blažena confessed, 'I've already had invitations to official Nazi functions, and I'm reluctant to go. So far, I've politely declined.'

'That could be a problem in itself, knowing that the Nazis regard you favourably,' Radek warned. 'Maybe you had better accept—it would be diplomatic, and might make things easier for us.'

Blažena considered. 'Well, if you think so, but I'm uncomfortable with it.'

* * *

For most Czechs, living under the German yoke was a heavy burden. Even though most resistance had been quashed, pockets remained. Then there was the Czechoslovak government-in-exile, based in London. It made the decision that Heydrich had to be dealt with. Two agents—Jan Kubiš, who was Czech, and Jozef Gabčík, who was Slovakian—heading a team trained by the British Special Operations Executive, were parachuted into Czechoslovakia. There they waited in hiding for an opportunity.

Fate played into their hands. On the twenty-seventh of May 1942, it was discovered that Heydrich had to fly to Berlin, after first checking in at his headquarters at Prague Castle. At a hairpin bend on the road in the Prague suburb of Libeň, the operatives waited for their chance. It came in the form of Heydrich, seated in his favourite car—a green open-topped Mercedes-Benz 320 Cabriolet B.

The car slowed to negotiate the bend. Gabčík tried to shoot, but his sub-machine gun jammed. Kubiš threw an anti-tank mine at the now-stationary car. It exploded under the rear wheel, sending fragments of steel and upholstery upwards, hitting Heydrich and wounding him. Both Heydrich and his driver Klein attempted to shoot their attackers, but Klein lost sight of them, and Heydrich collapsed in the road. He was taken to the nearby Bulovka Hospital. On examination, it was found he had sustained injuries to his diaphragm, spleen and lung, as well as a fractured rib. He fell in and out of fevers due to the contamination of the bomb fragments.

His old comrade Heinrich Himmler visited him. Heydrich appeared to be quoting poetry.

'Do you understand what he's saying? Is he delirious?' the attending doctor queried.

Himmler shook his head. 'No—I think he's quoting some lines from one of his father's operas.' He shook his head sadly. 'He's speaking about our inability to control our fate.'

Heydrich realised his end was coming, and succumbed to his injuries on the fourth of June. The Butcher of Prague was dead.

CHAPTER EIGHTEEN

When the news of Heydrich's death circulated, blind fear descended on Prague like a paralysis. There was no doubt that there would be a terrible reprisal.

'It's good that Heydrich is gone, but what will be the price?' Alex was despondent. 'Hitler won't let this go unpunished, even though the resistance fighters ended up committing suicide in the crypt of Saints Cyril and Methodius Cathedral after being betrayed.' He shook his head in despair. 'But that won't be enough.'

* * *

Just over a week from the day Heydrich was assassinated, Blažena was at home in her apartment reviewing the last pages of her script for *A Country Girl* when there came a tremendous pounding on her door. Startled, she dropped her script and debated whether to answer it or not.

'Blažena! It's us!' Alex's voice was stressed.

Blažena hurried to open the door, only for Alex and Ludmilla to stumble in, Alex supporting a half-fainting Ludmilla.

'What on earth—' Blažena rushed to assist, helping Ludmilla to sit on a sofa. She raised her eyes to Alex, who, with tears streaming from closed eyes, could only shake his head from side to side. Ludmilla, her face a mask of despair, was distraught and shaking—far removed from her tall, elegant self.

'Lidice, Lidice—my family!' was all she could utter, before dissolving into tears.

Blažena raised her eyes to Alex for enlightenment.

He took a deep breath. 'We knew there would be a reprisal of some sort. At first, Hitler wanted a random ten thousand Czech men executed, but was persuaded that it could mean the loss of valuable labour. So'— he put a protective arm around a sobbing Ludmilla,—'the Gestapo acted on false information and focused on Lidice.' His voice shook. 'They shot almost two hundred men and boys. Most of the women were sent to camps. Some children were selected for Germanisation, but over eighty were gassed. Then—' Here Alex almost broke down himself, '—they burned and razed Lidice to the ground. There's nothing left of it. Nothing at all.'

'Dear God!' Blažena raised her hand to a mouth wide-open with horror. Her mind blocked any rational thought and could only focus on what this meant. It meant not only the loss of Ludmilla's family, but also her aunt Vera and her mother Ivanka's sister, as well as her own cousins. She embraced Ludmilla, rocking her gently as if she were a child.

When she was capable of coherent speech, she whispered, 'Alex, what can we do?'

'Absolutely nothing,' Alex was grim. 'The horror has happened, and we must deal with it as best we can.'

Alex was right, of course, but Blažena considered it would take a long time, if ever, for Ludmilla to accept the loss of her entire family. It was Blažena's family, too, for that matter. All they could do would be to support her as best they could.

'I don't know how anyone could recover from something like this,' Blažena confided to Radek a few weeks later. 'They're monsters.'

'Yes, they are,' Radek agreed, 'and it didn't stop there. Just recently the SS found a radio transmitter at Ležaky, another village. The same thing happened.'

Blažena groaned. 'Sometimes all one wants to do is hide from it all, if that were possible.'

'Would you like to do that?' Radek was sympathetic. 'Your work on *A Country Girl* is complete. It's over to post-production now. You could take a break.'

Blažena considered. 'I could go home for a while, when Ludmilla has recovered a bit. If she goes back to work it might even help her deal with it. And there's another thing—Josef has been gone for some years now. I need some closure. I'm wondering if I can change my status. I think Josef could be declared legally dead.'

'That would make you a widow,' Radek thought for a moment. 'Or you could petition for divorce, citing desertion. You could always ask. I don't think the current régime would care. We can make inquiries if you like.'

* * *

It was strange at first living in her Rakovník home. Being widowed was strange, too. The Gestapo hadn't cared either way, and had accepted the files she had submitted over Josef's disappearance. She had shut up the Prague apartment, bringing Gizela, who was devoted to Zdenka. Gradually, she made and renewed acquaintances and settled into a relaxed way of life.

Once, she gazed from her front window to the house with the sgraffito decoration across the street. She sighed, thinking of the lovely Kafka House in Prague's Old Town Square, but now she felt that the city had been besmirched by the German occupation.

She was perturbed to find that she was still under the Nazi eye when a smart grey Mercedes-Benz W31 open tourer drew up outside her house one day. An adjutant in a crisp grey uniform and high peaked cap knocked on the door. He removed the cap, putting it under his arm.

'*Fräulein Blažena*, you are invited to a function at the Sports Hall.' He smiled and handed her the invitation. He replaced his cap. '*Heil Hitler*!' He turned on his heel and departed.

Blažena closed the door behind him and leant against it, clutching the invitation. *There's no question that I might not accept this. It's just assumed that I will.* She felt some unease. *Now I'll be seen to be consorting with the enemy through no fault of my own, and there's nothing I can do about it. This is a small place, and I'll soon be the talk of the town.*

* * *

She hadn't really meant to step on his foot. It was purely an accident, queuing in the butcher's shop for meat. Rationing meant queuing for everything these days. Blažena had just stepped back, to be greeted by an 'Ouch!' delivered in a deep voice. She whirled around to apologise, forced to look up to see a pleasant smiling man whose grey eyes returned a quizzical gaze.

'I'm terribly sorry!' Blažena was all confusion.

The man lifted his hat politely. 'That's all right, no harm done—I think—but before I go home and count my toes, might we have a coffee to celebrate this, er, encounter? By the way, my name is Zdenek Brodsky.'

Blažena lowered her face to hide the blush.

'It's fine if you don't want to,' he said, raising a placatory hand.

Blažena hesitated. 'No—I mean yes—that would be nice, but I really insist on paying.' Then she added, 'and I'm Blažena Kozlová,' surprising herself at using Josef's name with no emotion or regret.

It was very strange, Blažena reflected, to be having this conversation with a total stranger. Up until now, she had mostly been in the company of people she knew. A brief frisson of panic came over her, but she found it oddly easy to talk to this man with his quiet manner and his steady grey eyes.

* * *

'Well, how do I look?' Blažena twisted at the bodice of her costume, showing the dress to her advantage. She was wearing one of her best film costumes, sure that it would attract attention.

Gizela looked it over with a critical eye. 'It fits perfectly.'

'You look just like a fairy princess!' Zdenka was more fulsome with her praise.

'Thanks, both of you,' Blažena acknowledged, with a frown. 'I'm really nervous about this. I would much rather not be associating with these people. I'm only doing it for Radek and the studio.'

* * *

At the appointed hour, the same Mercedes-Benz drew up, and the smart adjutant escorted her down the steps and into the car. Out of the corner of her eye, Blažena could see some curtains twitching in the street. *Well, let them twitch. And, after the twitching, the tongues will start wagging. Well, let them wag. It's out of my control. I'm just acting a part, that's all.*

The Sports Hall was a blaze of lights, with the familiar blood-red Nazi banners lit from below. Blažena was escorted up the stairs, to be met by her host. He was very tall, with blond, close-cropped hair and intense cornflower-blue eyes set in a handsome face. Blažena was drawn to the dimple in his chin.

'As the *Oberführer* for this region, *Fräulein Blažena*, I welcome you to our function this evening,' her host greeted her. He smiled almost shyly. 'I have to say that I'm an ardent admirer of your film work, and tonight you are to be our guest of honour.'

Blažena inclined her head. 'Thank you,' she murmured, accepting his arm as he guided her towards a drink and food buffet. She accepted a champagne, but didn't drink any.

She looked around her. The hall was a sea of grey uniforms interspersed by the colours of the women's dresses. This was obviously an official function, judging by the formal atmosphere. The Oberführer guided her around the room, making introductions to stony-eyed officers and their wives, and to local dignitaries who had been selected to attend. It was obvious he took his duties as host very seriously.

'One has to do this at these functions,' he smiled apologetically, 'but when I'm not the *Oberführer*, my name is Helmut von Neumann, and I look forward to a closer acquaintance.' He made a formal bow.

Blažena sketched a small curtsy in return, but her mind was racing. This was a dangerously attractive and powerful man. She would have to draw a very fine line indeed.

* * *

She was not overly surprised to see Gizela and Zdenka still up and waiting for her return. When the car had arrived and the same smart adjutant had delivered her to the front door, they were eager with questions.

Blažena sank into an armchair, pulling at the skirt of her dress irritably. 'I'm too tired to tell you everything about it,' she confessed. 'I only know that it was a dreadful atmosphere, with Nazi uniforms everywhere, and town dignitaries bowing and scraping. The women were glaring at me, and the men were ogling me, while the Germans just stood around in their shiny boots looking superior. I felt like a slab of meat in a butcher's shop!' She shuddered. 'And that *Oberführer*, von Neumann—I'm going to have to be very careful there. He could prove a very dangerous man. I feel I'm treading on a precipice. One false step, and I'm over the edge.'

CHAPTER NINETEEN

Oberführer Helmut von Neumann continued to pay court, with invitations to small receptions and musical soirées. Blažena had no option but to accept these with as good a grace as she could muster, and interpreted them as an attempt by the Germans to present a human face to their invasion. The *Oberführer* had taken her aside during one of these functions, in order to speak with her privately.

'*Fräulein Blažena*, I wondered if we could speak of your excellent work in films. I know I mentioned that I was an admirer, but I would really like to learn the processes you must go through to achieve your high standard of acting.'

Blažena, who had been very nervous at his request for a private conversation, was slightly relieved. 'I believe it's all a matter of preparation,' she responded. 'I do study the screenplays very thoroughly. But'—she paused for a moment—'learning the script is the mechanical part. That's the dialogue, and also the blocking—that's where I imagine my character is going to move. Of course'—she smiled—'that is also down to the director, and his requirements, and I have a most sensitive director in Radek Novotny.'

'But, *Fräulein*,' Oberführer Helmut von Neumann persisted, 'whatever you do seems so natural.'

Blažena thought for a moment, then replied, 'That's when I really enter the character—I try to actually become the person, with all that drives them towards their actions.'

'Ah.' Von Neumann thought for a minute. 'It seems your approach is very psychological.'

Blažena smiled. 'Why, yes, I believe it is, and it works very well for me.'

Blažena breathed more freely, relieved when von Neumann nodded his satisfaction and they returned to the party. She knew that when the evening was over, she would be driven back home in the same car, and that would give rise to even more gossip. She was already aware of some sideways glances she received when she was out in the town. *I'm sure my reputation is in tatters, but this is all about survival. It's war, after all.*

* * *

She tried to analyse the *Oberführer*'s relationship with her and came to the conclusion that, as an educated German officer, he admired her for her undeniable beauty and acting reputation, and her availability as a companion. She had to assume that he was unmarried, for otherwise he would be accompanied by his wife to formal occasions. She also had to respect his code of ethics, for he never once overstepped the boundaries of polite social behaviour. Still, there was the issue of reciprocating and maintaining that polite behaviour with one who was, technically, the enemy.

On the other hand, Blažena was surprised and pleased at how smoothly her relationship with Zdenek was progressing since their chance encounter when she accidentally trod on his foot. It was a comfortable awareness of each other's personalities and characters. Zdenek was interested up to a point in Blažena's film career, but not really a fan of the cinema. Zdenek's profession was in apartment construction, something quite alien to Blažena's range of interests.

'Do you mean to say you wouldn't come to see one of my films if it screened here?' Blažena teased one day.

Zdenek grinned. 'Well, I might,' he considered. 'That is, if you would like a tour of one of my construction sites.'

Blažena pulled a face. 'We might leave things as they are,' she conceded.

In spite of this, or maybe because of it, their relationship developed calmly, with none of the passion and drama of her fiery romance with Josef.

* * *

A phone call from Radek asking to visit aroused her curiosity, but she knew she would be very pleased to see him again.

'So—you've come all this way just to say hello?' she teased when they both were comfortable with coffee in her sitting room.

Radek had a conspiratorial look. 'No, not just to say hello,' he admitted. 'More to suggest that you think about another film.'

Blažena sat up. This was a surprise. 'Do you mean to say you're still permitted to work?'

Radek looked serious. 'Rumour has it that the war is not going too well for the Nazis,' he confided quietly. 'Apparently, they want another morale-booster like *A Country Girl*. They would like you to do it.'

Blažena felt the old excitement bubbling up at the thought of working again, and also the prospect of being in Prague once more. This was countered by the possibility of having to work under the eye of Nazi censors, even though Radek would be directing, and would mentor her.

'I'm not so sure,' she murmured, 'I hope it doesn't mean that I might encounter that dreadful Joseph Goebbels again. He really gave me the horrors when I was working on *A Country Girl!*'

Radek tried to reassure her. 'As far as I know, Goebbels is back in Berlin, supervising other propaganda and feature films being made at Babelsberg Studios. It's where Riefenstahl made *Triumph of the Will* in 1935,' he reminded her, pressing his case. 'The Germans are still using Babelsberg in spite of their worry about the possibility of Allied air raids.'

Blažena relaxed. 'Well, that does ease my concern somewhat,' she admitted. 'Very well, if you want me, I'll do it. I trust you.'

* * *

Going to Prague to work on a new film would mean distancing herself from Oberführer von Neumann, and would be a good excuse to remove herself from his attentions. Unhappily, it would also mean being away from Zdenek.

'I may have to go to Prague again,' she confided to Zdenek some days later. 'They want me to make another film.' She waited for his reaction.

He considered for a moment. 'I will miss you very much,' he admitted, 'but I think our friendship will survive. It won't be for too long, I imagine.'

'I would hope not.' She didn't like the thought of being separated, but her work had priority. She felt that her actions sometimes had to be made in the context of pleasing other people as well as herself.

'Would you like to be in Prague for a while?' she asked Zdenka soon after.

Zdenka looked thoughtful, head on one side. 'It would be really nice. I could see Aunty Ludmilla and Uncle Alex again. I miss them. You do too, don't you?'

Blažena smiled. 'Yes, darling, I do miss them a lot. It will be lovely to see them again.'

Once settled in the Prague apartment, Blažena wasted no time in contacting Ludmilla, who seemed almost pathetically relieved to see her. Ludmilla appeared almost to be her old self, although there was an underlying sadness in her eyes. 'I can't give up hope completely,' she confessed, 'in case any of the children from Lidice who survived might be related to me. I did have nieces and nephews there. You had family there too, for that matter.' Her trembling mouth betrayed her tight smile, and it broke Blažena's heart.

'There's always a chance, and we must hope for the best,' Blažena sympathised, although privately she thought the chance to be a slim one.

* * *

Prague still bore the marks of the occupiers. Nazi uniforms and the black coats of plain-clothed agents were everywhere, and most people looked gaunt and weary—the result of constant fear and lack of food. Even though it was early spring, and the desiccated leaves of winter were being scattered along the Vltava embankment by brisk breezes under a pale blue sky, the sense of oppression hung like a suffocating vapour.

Blažena forced herself to focus on the new project and consumed the script for *Victory for the Country*, determined to complete her part as quickly as possible. She went up to Barrandov only when absolutely necessary, hating to use the dirty trams, and taking personal offence at the tram stops being announced in German as well as Czech.

The atmosphere at Barrandov under the Deutsche Prag-Film was uneasy, even though work was proceeding on Goebbels' three new sound studios. Harried-looking production staff worked urgently to churn out mostly propaganda films to bolster the German war effort, alongside a small number of feature films. To Blažena, Radek's earlier comment putting a Nazi victory into question seemed justified.

He was all admiration for Blažena's approach to the new project. 'You mean to say you've memorised your part already?' he queried soon after she arrived in Prague. 'We don't even have our shooting schedule yet!'

'I want to get this done as quickly as possible,' Blažena argued, 'and my role as a shrewd factory worker uncovering a clandestine plot against the Reich is rather straightforward. When it's shot, I can go home again. The war seems further away there. And, I miss my friend Zdenek.'

'Aha!' Radek was all ears. 'Tell me more!'

'Well, he's a nice, calm person. I think he's just what I need at this time.' She considered. 'I think he's very good for me.'

Radek smiled. 'Well, if he makes you happy, you have my blessing. You deserve it, if anyone does.'

Being absent from Zdenek made Blažena consider that he did indeed make her happy, in a calm and restful way, and determined to strengthen their relationship when she returned home. This would be possible in a few weeks, when she had shot all her scenes in *Victory for the Country*. She no longer had any interest in being part of the post-production, content to leave it to the team of editors and effects people.

Working under censorship had stripped the creative joy of film-making for her, and it was reduced to something mechanical. *Will working ever be the same again for me? Can I ever transform myself into my characters the way I used to?* Blažena pondered on where life and events had taken her, and how they had formed her. *Whatever happened to my young self, when all I ever wanted to do was to become a creation of fantasy?* She reluctantly accepted that those heady days were now behind her, and that living in the shadow of war made any kind of future impossible to predict.

CHAPTER TWENTY

Back in Rakovník, Blažena was able to relax. The large square was attractive in spring, with its trees now in leaf and garden beds lively with blooms. The Town Hall glowed in its pink tones, while the buildings at the end of the square contrasted in pastel colours. The Slavia building, easily identified by its name in Art Deco lettering, was the standout, with bright green banding its red brick façade and eaves. All the colours seemed to lend an air of gaiety, in sharp contrast to the drabness of Prague. The invader's presence seemed non-existent here, which made it the ideal place to wind down.

Working on *Victory for the Country* had not been a difficult shoot, as it was a straightforward narrative, but in Prague, she could not escape the feeling of oppression. Here, she was able to resume friendships from her youth and take in the passing parade, including the few Jewish people, identified by the yellow stars they were forced to wear sewn onto their clothing. It reminded Blažena forcibly of those shops in Prague that had been boarded up and their owners mysteriously disappearing. That was the only discordant note to mar the peaceful atmosphere.

* * *

'So—was working on a film again exciting?' Zdenek queried one day over lunch, which was a meagre affair thanks to wartime rationing. 'Was it like old times?'

'Frankly, no.' Blažena was adamant. 'The atmosphere at Barrandov is depressing—not at all like pre-war times, when the feeling was challenging and creative. Before the Germans took control, everyone seemed positive. There was a happy atmosphere, from the set designers and constructors right through to the on-set crews and actors.'

'Working on this film was a real challenge to keeping my spirits up and committing to the part. It was a great relief to get away from all the gloom.'

Zdenek laid his knife down and contemplated the checked tablecloth. He looked up and took Blažena's hand. 'Well, why don't we talk about something closer to home, like our relationship? Have you thought about it at all?'

'I've thought about it a lot,' Blažena replied. 'Actually, I've thought about little else these past few weeks.'

Zdenek grimaced. 'Is that a good thing or a bad thing?'

Blažena put her other hand into his. 'It's a very good thing,' she murmured, blushing a little.

'I'm a little past getting down on one knee, so would it be all right if I proposed to you as we are, across the table? Will you marry me? Will you become Paní Brodsková?' Zdenek's manner was light-hearted, but Blažena saw in his questioning grey eyes just how serious he was.

Blažena's blue-grey eyes locked with his steady gaze. 'It would be absolutely fine. I would like to marry you very much,' she answered, surprising herself at how easy it was to say the words. The deep wound left by Josef's disappearance had largely healed, and Blažena had forced herself to move on, willing her mind not to dwell on that part of her life. For her, Josef's character remained an enigma. It was as if that part of her life remained a terrible dream, apart from the existence of her beautiful daughter.

Zdenek grinned his delight at her acceptance. 'We will be apart from time to time,' he admitted, 'because my construction work takes me away for periods of weeks or more.'

Blažena shrugged. 'Well, I may have to be away if they want me to work in other films,' she said, 'so I guess that makes us even.' She smiled broadly. 'We'll make it work.'

Maybe it was because Zdenek had been called away on construction work and she was uncertain about her life-changing decision to accept his proposal, but Blažena was not her normal self and wondered later what madness made her do what she did.

She was walking home after shopping, her mind full of plans for her and Zdenek's future, when she heard a commotion in the distance behind her. She turned around to see a covered army truck, with soldiers in the dreaded grey uniform shouting and forcing people from their houses and up into the back of the vehicle. Women were screaming, and the strident sounds of crying children rose above the tumult. For a moment, Blažena thought her eyes and ears were deceiving her. Horrified, she noticed Michaela Horáková, a woman she knew from shopping at the local delicatessen, trying to persuade two little boys to run in her direction.

Without thinking, Blažena grabbed their hands along with her shopping bags and fled as if the Devil himself was at her heels. She whirled around the corner into her street and continued, half-dragging, half-carrying the boys, and didn't stop until she was pounding on the door of her house. A startled Gizela opened the door and stood back as Blažena burst in with the children and slammed the door. She leant against it, breathless.

'What—?' Gizela gasped, her eyes wide with fright.

'They—they were going to take them!' Blažena was desperately trying to control her breathing. 'Mrs Goldmann's little boys—soldiers are taking people from their homes. Michaela Horáková made Mrs Goldmann's children run—to me!'

'What will happen?' Gizela was aghast. 'Did anyone see you?' The younger boy was crying softly. His elder brother just stood regarding the women with wide, terrified eyes.

'I don't think so, but I had to do something,' Desperation forced Blažena to defend her actions. 'We can hide them in the second cellar. Those dreadful soldiers mustn't find them!'

Gizela looked terrified. 'But how can we keep them here? Someone is sure to find out!'

Blažena thought, desperate to formulate a logical plan. 'Obviously, they can't go out, and we must find things for them to do. We must be careful with shopping—too much food at a time will look suspicious.'

They embarked on their secretive mission. The elder of the children understood the

gravity of the situation, and ensured that his little brother realised the danger they were in.

Blažena stressed the secrecy they all had to observe. 'Jacob,' she said, addressing the elder of the two, 'you understand how quiet you must be, all the time, don't you?'

The boy nodded, and Eli, his younger brother, automatically mimicked him. 'We understand,' promised Jacob. But then he looked questioningly at Blažena.

'Why are the Germans doing this to us?' he queried. 'We haven't done anything to hurt them.'

Tears formed on Blažena's cheeks. 'I know, darling,' she murmured, 'But there are some people who are persuaded to hate others, and there's very little we can do about it.'

Jacob frowned. 'But why would they want to take Mother and Father away? They are good people. They haven't hurt anyone.'

'I don't know,' Blažena could barely speak for the lump in her throat. 'I just don't know. I only know that for now, for your safety, you must do exactly as we tell you. We must make it a kind of game, but a serious one.'

Jacob nodded seriously, and little Eli nodded, too, but held his brother's hand tightly

* * *

Nerves stretched like violin strings whenever anyone rang the doorbell or came to visit. They went shopping separately, hoping that no-one would notice the increased amount of food being purchased. Blažena dared to hope that her impulsive action had not been in vain, but it was not to be. One week later the front door resonated to a tremendous hammering. A nervous Gizela opened it to be confronted by Oberführer von Neumann. His face was white with anger, his blue eyes wide open and blazing.

'Where are they?' he hissed in a voice tight with fury. He turned on Blažena, one hand raised to prevent her speaking. 'No—don't deny it! We know they are here. How could you do such a stupid thing? You have put yourselves and those children at risk, and even I will have much difficulty in trying to protect you!' His voice softened. 'You must know that we have rules in place for those people. There are places for them. The children will go to a special camp—Theresien- stadt. You call it Terezín, I believe. They have special programs for children—music and art. That is why you must give them up to me, now. You really must.'

The *Oberführer*'s voice was firm but soft, and Blažena almost felt that she could detect a sense of entreaty. He was trying to make the dreadful situation as gentle as possible. Blažena had no words to defend her actions, and they had no option but to obey.

She sank down on her knees to hug each child in turn, her eyes brimming with tears. When von Neumann and a soldier had left with the children, Blažena sank down in a chair and sobbed as if her heart would break. *What kind of world do I live in where innocent children can be sucked into the maw of a dreadful régime?* Seeing the children in their plight had brought to mind Ludmilla's grief and the horrors of Lidice and Ležaky.

When she could think rationally, she realised the insanity of her actions. *Did I think I was one of my film heroines, to act in such a reckless way? That I could just spirit them away, and we would all be safe?* She had just acted on impulse and in the ordinary way of things, would, along with Gizela and the children, be on her way in a covered truck to God knows where, and to an unknown fate. She shuddered to think of it. She thanked her lucky stars for her odd relationship with Oberführer von Neumann. *If it had been anyone else, things would have gone very badly for us.*

CHAPTER TWENTY-ONE

It took some time for Blažena to recover from the disastrous repercussions of her impulsive deed. She told herself that it had been stupid and risky, but her sense of morality told her that her instinct was correct. She steeled herself to confess the episode to Zdenek, who was horrified.

'That was unsafe and foolish! It could have ended very badly,' he argued, 'but I understand your compassion for the children. And what about this von Neumann? Why haven't I heard about him?'

Blažena felt she had to explain the situation. 'I suppose you could call him a film enthusiast, and for some reason he admires my work. There's nothing romantic in it.' She was acutely aware of Zdenek's raised eyebrows. 'Really, he's always been very gentlemanly towards me, and thanks to his admiration, I got off very lightly from the situation. It could have been worse—much worse.'

She frowned. 'You see, for some reason, Goebbels seems to see me as a good model of Aryan womanhood and that's why I had to play those roles.' She shrugged. 'So, you must understand that I can't very well refuse to cooperate in these situations. I might even have to do more films like that to keep the Nazis happy. Our work is precarious enough as it is.'

Zdenek was not best pleased at the predicament she was in, but reluctantly accepted things as they were. For her part, Blažena felt it was time to try to put it all away and focus on her immediate future. She phoned Ludmilla to tell her of Zdenek's proposal and her acceptance, and invited her and Alex to Rakovník for their wedding. She also contacted Radek, who was delighted and accepted happily.

She knew that Gizela had accepted Zdenek and liked him, and so the only stumbling block was Zdenka, who by now was old enough to hold strong views on everything.

'Would you like Uncle Zdenek to be your new father?' she asked one day.

Zdenka considered, head on one side as usual. 'Yes—I like him very much. I really can't remember Daddy since he went away and never came back, because I was just a little girl.'

Zdenka's response brought tears to Blažena's eyes as she remembered times past. But that's just what they were—times past—and now it was necessary to think of the future.

Ludmilla, Alex and Radek arrived in due time and were introduced to Zdenek. To Blažena's delight, they approved of him, for she valued their opinions as long-standing friends.

* * *

The wedding was a simple affair at the local registry office in the Town Hall, in keeping with the challenging times. Blažena wore her best day dress, and her precious locket gleamed on her bosom. Ludmilla was a very glamorous bridesmaid, and a proud Radek acted the part of giving Blažena away. Zdenek had found a colleague who acted as best man, and Blažena thought Zdenek and his friend looked splendid in their suits. She had never seen Zdenek wearing a suit, and he looked a very romantic figure, which warmed Blažena's heart even more. Gizela and Zdenka made up the party, and a beaming Zdenka carried Blažena's bridal bouquet.

After the documents were signed, they all went for a celebratory dinner at the Slavia, one of the few restaurants still operating. During the meal, Blažena caught Ludmilla and Alex holding hands. *It's about time that they cemented their relationship.* She resolved to help things along. *They're two lovely people. Maybe they're just afraid of commitment.*

A knock on the door brought Gizela. Her hand flew to her mouth in surprise and fear as she saw the figure standing there.

'May I see *Fräulein Blažena*?' asked Oberführer von Neumann politely.

Gizela struggled to maintain her composure. 'Ye—yes, of course,' she stuttered, and fled in search of Blažena, who she found in the sitting room stitching a dress for Zdenka.

'It's that German,' she whispered. 'He wants to see you for some reason.'

Blažena started up. 'What on earth would he want to see me for?' She still had conflicting emotions from her actions in trying to save the children, and felt guilty from her previous encounter with the *Oberführer*. Plucking up her courage, she went to the door.

'*Fräulein Blažena*,' he said, bowing politely. 'Or rather, I should say, Frau Brodsková, since I understand you are married. My congratulations.'

'Th—thank you, that is very kind of you,' Blažena replied. 'How may I help you?'

The *Oberführer* looked a little embarrassed. 'I'm aware of how upset you were over those Jewish children,' he explained, 'and I wondered if you might wish to visit them. I am told that they are in a special section of Terezín,' he added, as if it explained everything, 'and I could, if you wish, arrange for you to see them.' Conflicting emotions flickered across his face. 'You must know we had no choice but to send them there, but I thought ….'

He left the sentence hanging, while Blažena considered what he had just said. 'Y—yes, I think I would like to,' she said. 'And about their parents—?'

The *Oberführer* looked down. 'I really can't say—I don't know where they are,' he confessed, 'but, as I said, if you would like to visit the children—'

Blažena had made her decision. 'Thank you, yes, I would like that. If you can let me know a day, I will be ready to go.'

Oberführer von Neumann looked relieved. 'Very well, I shall contact you and advise a time. My adjutant will drive you there.' He bowed politely again, and returned to his waiting car.

* * *

'Who would have thought he would offer a thing like that?' mused Blažena later. 'Is there such a thing as a good German?'

Gizela shrugged. 'Maybe, but I think they're few and far between. Maybe it's just because he admires your film work so much.'

Blažena considered. 'I almost regret accepting the offer,' she said, 'but I'd really like to see for myself.'

'I've heard that they have cultural programs there,' Gizela sounded optimistic. 'It could prove to be a nice place. You won't know unless you see it for yourself.'

The *Oberführer's* advice came a couple of weeks later, and Blažena prepared herself for the journey. The Terezín camp was roughly thirty miles from Rakovník, and she hoped that the road wouldn't be too bad, and that checkpoint delays wouldn't hold them up.

* * *

A knock brought Blažena, dressed in a costume suitable for travel, to the door. The *Oberführer*'s adjutant stood waiting. He gave her a little bow. She indicated that she needed a moment to pack something to take. Not knowing what would be appropriate, she had prepared a basket of provisions—fruit, bread, and some cheeses. As the car moved off into a cold, fog-shrouded morning, she had mixed feelings. *Why do I want to see the children? Wouldn't it be better just to try to forget the incident?* But something nagged at her. She needed to know their fate, and to know just what the Germans were doing.

When they arrived at Terezín, the adjutant got out and opened the door for her. He indicated that she was to follow him to the Commandant's office, where he produced a folded note to the officer. The Commandant, a squat man with dull, slate-grey eyes and a bad complexion, looked at her curiously, shrugged and gestured for her to follow him. As they reached the inner fortress entrance, the fog lifted slightly and she noted the text *Arbeit Macht Frei* above the gate.

'What does that mean?' she queried. The Commandant, who knew some Czech, turned to her.

His thin, bloodless lips twisted in a leer. *'Work makes you free,'* he translated.

Blažena stared in dismay. Rows of gloomy brick barracks crowded in from all directions, surrounded by high walls topped with barbed wire. There was no sign of activity—no music, laughing, or the sounds of children playing. The odour of unwashed bodies filled her nostrils, but over all rose the reek of despair.

The Commandant stopped at one door and barked something. 'The children,' he muttered.

Two skeletal figures shuffled out of the door. Blažena couldn't believe her eyes. The boys, dressed in rags, looked up at her with enormous, unseeing eyes.

Blažena fought to control her emotions. 'Eli, Jacob, I have brought you something,' she murmured in Czech. 'Something nice.' She put the basket on the ground in front of them. 'Look—there are some lovely cherries and plums, and other things to eat.' The boys stared at the basket uncomprehendingly.

'Aren't you hungry?' Blažena pleaded. She knelt down before them. 'Surely you would like to eat some of this nice food?'

The children just continued to stare at the basket, then raised their eyes again to hers without any recognition or emotion.

'You do understand me, don't you?' she begged. 'This lovely food is just for you. Please enjoy it.'

There was no response from the children. They just stood like small, tattered statues.

On the verge of tears Blažena rose, her legs trembling. She turned to the Commandant, her voice breaking. 'Please, may we go?'

They walked back to the car. The fog by now had changed to a grey drizzle of rain. Blažena followed the Commandant blindly, her eyes full of tears. The adjutant gave her a sympathetic glance as he opened the car door. She sat staring straight ahead, clutching the chain of her locket as if she might break it, all the way back to Rakovník.

CHAPTER TWENTY-TWO

Blažena managed to retain her self-control until they reached Rakovník. When Gizela opened the door, she stumbled in and collapsed into an armchair. 'Gizela, it was terrible,' she moaned, trying not to break down. 'Those poor boys were starving. They didn't know me. They didn't understand that I had brought them some food. And that place—I could see the crowding, and the smell of all those poor people was appalling! They are kept in there like animals, but no-one would treat an animal like that!'

She shivered at the recollection. 'That frightful person in charge—a Commandant—he had a face like a toad, and I could feel he was sneering at me all the time!' She shuddered, then drew herself up with an effort. 'And that dreadful sign over the gate—*Arbeit Macht Frei*—what a ghastly deception! Now I know just what horrors the Reich is capable of, and the worst part is that most of those incarcerated there are

Czech.' She looked at Gizela unseeingly, her mind in turmoil. 'And if they can treat children like that, how much worse are they treating adults?'

Gizela was appalled. 'And if they're doing that in Terezín, they must be doing even worse in the other camps we hear about. We were told that Terezín is a model camp where everyone is treated well.'

'Well, that is obviously German propaganda, and for my part, it will change my relationship with von Neumann.' Blažena's lip curled in disgust. 'Even though his motive probably was based on kindness, I don't know if I can bear to see him anymore. It's difficult to know if he's aware of the conditions there. I feel he's a good German trapped in a very bad system. Maybe he's a victim as much as anyone.'

Gizela pondered. 'Maybe you really can't blame him,' she reasoned. 'He's torn between trying to do his job properly, and trying to be kind to you. He's in a most difficult position.'

Blažena stared pensively into space for a moment, then she shuddered. 'It was dreadful, but I can't do anything about it. I only know that it's going to haunt my dreams for a very long time.'

Her shoulders relaxed. 'I have to try to think of happier things. Now Zdenek and I have to plan our future, including where we're going to live.'

* * *

That discussion, when Blažena and Zdenek had the chance to be together, was easily decided.

'You know my apartment is small.' Zdenek was thinking of how they both could live in his one-bedroom flat.

Blažena considered the situation. 'And my house has plenty of room for the two of us, and for Zdenka and Gizela as well. It makes more sense if my place becomes our base.'

Zdenek looked concerned. 'You're sure that will work? I wouldn't want to intrude on your household.'

'It's not an issue,' Blažena explained. 'Zdenka and Gizela have their own rooms, and we will have ours. There's plenty of space. So, it will become our household.'

They both agreed it was workable, and Zdenek suggested that he lease his apartment, to have it used and also for it to earn extra income, which would be welcome. Blažena wasn't concerned about finances, but there had not been any news from Radek about the possibility of another film.

* * *

When Radek spoke with Blažena on one of his visits to Rakovník, he intimated that production at Barrandov had slowed considerably. 'Word is that the tide of the war is turning,' he confided, 'and even Goebbels' propaganda output is not having the desired effect. News sometimes trickles through from the Resistance.'

He elaborated, in response to Blažena's querying look. 'Hitler's obsession with his *lebensraum* in the East, which was his attempted invasion of the Soviet Union, was a total disaster a couple of years ago.' Blažena was looking confused, so he explained. 'Hitler made the same mistake that Napoleon did—he didn't take into account the severity of the Russian winter. Apparently, Germany suffered more deaths in the Soviet Union than any other country. After a terrible battle, the Germans failed to take Stalingrad. And in France more recently,' he continued, 'the Allies had a success when they invaded Normandy. So, you see, things are not going Germany's way.'

Blažena was pensive. 'That means we virtually shut down, doesn't it? They won't want any more inspirational films like *Victory for the Country*, will they?'

'No.' Radek considered a moment, and then his bright blue eyes twinkled. 'But when things change, hopefully Deutsche Prag-Film will disappear, and Barrandov and Pragcine will be returned to us, and we can prepare to work again.'

* * *

As it happened, circumstances changed in a way that would mean no film-making in the near future for Blažena. Some months later, she felt the familiar nauseous feelings, accompanied by morning sickness. She was no longer in Prague, so a visit to Doctor Tomek was not possible. On Madame Rabasová's advice, she consulted a local doctor, Miroslav Vasko. Doctor Vasko confirmed what she had suspected. 'Yes, my dear,' he smiled, 'you are pregnant. Congratulations!'

Zdenek was delighted when Blažena told him. 'That's wonderful news!' he exclaimed. 'Our little family is growing.'

Blažena was pleased, but realised that having another child meant no filming for some time. She accepted that, for the foreseeable future, motherhood was to be her lot. This wasn't like before. *Then I was still working for months until I had Zdenka.* She wondered if she could cope with the inactivity. Previously she had been able to work on *Enduring Love* while she was pregnant. *I could lose my acting edge, and that would never do. Is motherhood my only future?* She had time in the following months to contemplate the future, but no resolutions presented themselves.

When her time came near, Blažena and Gizela consulted Marta Pribyl, who had delivered Zdenka, and Marta was happy to provide her services again. Zdenek managed to be home close to Blažena's time, and was overjoyed when she presented him with a healthy baby boy.

Zdenek had difficulty controlling his emotions. 'He's beautiful,' he murmured, looking down through tear-filled eyes at Blažena and her new child. 'What will we call him?'

Blažena smiled. Although she was very tired from the birth, she had very definite views on the matter. 'I thought we would call him Slava,' she said. 'It means "Glory", and although we're living in these terrible times, glorious days must come.'

The baby was clutching at Zdenek's finger. 'Slava—it's a perfect name for a lovely little boy—my little son,' he said softly, his words falling gently like a benediction on the tiny face looking up with wide-open deep blue eyes, and he kissed Blažena's forehead tenderly.

* * *

Unhappily, Blažena's optimism was unfounded. Radek's voice on the unreliable telephone line was scratchy and thin. 'At last, in 1945, the Czech Resistance here has encouraged Pragers to move against the Germans after Hitler threatened to destroy the capital,' Radek reported. 'Citizens here have destroyed German street signs. Tram conductors are refusing to collect fares in German currency, and won't announce tram stops in German. People are even setting up road barricades to impede German forces—what's left of them. The best news, though, is that Hitler is dead.'

'What?!' Blažena was thunderstruck. 'When? How?'

'Apparently his wife Eva Braun took a cyanide capsule, then Hitler shot himself on April thirtieth, in Berlin.'

'His wife?' Blažena was astonished. 'I didn't know he was married!'

'Very few people knew that,' Radek said. 'She was in Hitler's inner circle, but stayed at the *Berghof* in Bavaria as part of his household.'

Blažena was fascinated. 'Did she play any political part in Hitler's organisation?'

'No,' Radek replied, 'and it was only near the end that she actually went to Berlin. By then, Hitler had retreated to the Fűhrerbunker under the Reich Chancellery.'

'What do you mean by the end?'

'It's really ironic,' Radek said. 'They married in the bunker less than four days before they died, even while the Soviet troops were forcing their way into the city centre.'

Blažena was elated. 'But if Hitler's dead, that should mean the war is over!' she exclaimed.

'Not necessarily,' answered Radek. 'Some German forces are so devoted to the Nazi doctrine that they are fighting on, and now word is that the Soviet forces may be advancing in our direction.'

'At least the Germans know the tide has turned against them. Surely that's a good thing!' Blažena was elated.

'Not necessarily.' Radek's voice was sombre. 'The United States forces were gaining control in our direction, but their General George Patton might have to stop at the city of Plzeň.'

Blažena was indignant. 'Why would he have to do that? The Americans are democratic, aren't they? After all, they were fighting Hitler.' She laughed. 'And I know that Plzeň is noted for its wonderful Pilsner beer, but it couldn't be over that!'

'It's a devastating blow for us, but the American President Eisenhower sees Czechoslovakia as being in the Soviet sphere, according to the Yalta Conference,' Radek explained tiredly.

'What on earth is that?' Blažena queried, 'and how could it affect us?'

Radek sounded dispirited. 'In early February of this year there was a conference in Yalta in the Crimea—a meeting of the heads of state from the United States, the United Kingdom and the Soviet Union. It was agreed that our country was to be in the Soviet sphere. Heaven only knows what's going to happen to us now. Only the future will tell.' He said goodbye and hung up.

Blažena replaced the handset slowly, her brow furrowed in concern. *So, this is to be our future. Uncertainty for the fate of Barrandov, Radek's company and my acting career.* So much for her hope of glorious days for their new-born son. *Slava will grow up in an unpredictable world, and his prospects may be bleak.*

CHAPTER TWENTY-THREE

Radek had every right to be depressed. It had just turned May, and scattered German forces were still desperately trying to retain their grip on Prague, although that grip was loosening. People were wary of moving about too much, but Radek still met with Alex and Ludmilla in their apartment occasionally.

Alex's company was partly under flagging German control. He had managed to retain his position as publishing manager, although he chafed under the yoke of the SS who had been using the company mostly for propaganda leaflets.

'Do you think we'll ever be able to get back to normal?' Alex entreated his superior.

Miloš, his company manager and direct superior, was quietly optimistic. 'Their activities are definitely slowing down,' he acknowledged, 'and they seem more confused than anything, as if they've lost their focus. At least we can hope to return to our normal kind of production, and not those dreadful images we had to print. I think we'll survive.'

Unfortunately, Ludmilla was now without any work as the government, still in the hands of the occupiers, was in a shambles, and they were living hand-to-mouth in her Bartolomějská Street apartment. Stress had caused Ludmilla to lose the glow of her beauty, but her dark brown eyes still shone with intensity.

'You know that Blažena's had her baby.' Radek had been in constant touch with Blažena during her pregnancy.

'Yes,' Ludmilla smiled, 'a lovely little boy. She must be very happy with him, and Zdenek must be a proud father.'

'True,' interjected Alex, 'but Blažena is concerned about the future as we all are, and Zdenek is worrying about his position in construction, because the economy is in tatters.'

Radek grimaced. 'They have every right to worry, with things in the current state. I didn't tell Blažena, but since last year, leftist-oriented Czech filmmakers have been pressuring for Barrandov to be nationalised. Apparently, it has been approved in principle by the Czech government-in-exile in Britain. If it happens, all the film companies working at Barrandov will lose their businesses. That will include my company, Pragcine. You know that Miloš Havel was forced by the Nazis to sell his share in Barrandov Studios, and was lucky to remain as manager?'

'At least he was able to retain a position of sorts,' murmured Ludmilla.

'Yes—but working under the Nazis could be a poisoned chalice when the smoke clears from their control. I was able to keep working as manager of Pragcine because Goebbels wanted to use Blažena in those "patriotic films".' Radek put air quotes around the phrase. He sounded pessimistic. 'It could put me in an unenviable position, too.' He sighed. 'Anyway, it doesn't augur well for the film industry here. And there's some news—there was some damage to the Barrandov buildings. Apparently, some Pragers were resisting. The Germans are not having it all their way!'

His expression lightened. 'And just yesterday, the radio was broadcasting in Czech and not German! They pulled the Nazi flag down and raised the Czecho-slovak and American flags!'

He grinned broadly. 'Even though the Waffen-SS were posted inside the building, the Czech Radio staff managed to remove the room signs so that the Germans weren't able to find the newsroom. Our Czech police units stormed the building, and there was a fierce gun battle. Eventually, the Germans were forced from the building. Later, even when the Germans damaged the building by bombing it, the resistance kept transmitting first in Strašnice, and later from St Nicholas Church in the Old Town Square, playing Czech music, announcing the Nazis had lost, and calling on all Czechs to rise up. Three days later, the Czech Radio building's equipment was repaired, and the staff returned to continue broadcasting!'

Radek spread his hands wide in a gesture of satisfaction. 'That was a wonderful gesture of our defiance, and it's so good for our morale! But it came at a cost—many resistance fighters and Czech police were killed. But as is always the case in war, any resistance activity pays a terrible price. And it's really odd'—Radek shook his head in disbelief—'our civilians, led by our Czech resistance, were joined by a group called the Russian Liberation Army. Can you believe that? The Germans tried to counter-attack, but civilians cleverly constructed barricades at strategic points around the city, which deterred them.'

Ludmilla had her doubts about this hand-to-hand fighting. 'Was there any major retaliation, from either side?' she demanded bluntly.

Radek shrugged, and sadness passed over his face. 'Yes—the Germans used civilian Czechs as human shields, but unfortunately, we Czechs took revenge against German civilians, encouraged by the Czech government-in-exile.' He sighed. 'It seems everyone loses some of their humanity in war.'

'That's so true.' Ludmilla's tone was bitter. Her memories of Lidice still haunted her, and she felt it would be a long time before she could forgive that atrocity. She would never forget.

* * *

It was a little later, after Radek had left. 'It's still only afternoon, so do you think we could go out for a walk somewhere?' Alex was feeling buoyed by Radek's news. 'We can check to see if it's safe.'

Ludmilla thought it was a good idea. 'But only if we don't see any Germans,' she insisted, 'we don't want to run into trouble.'

They ventured out, avoiding larger avenues and wandered through safe back streets as far as Železná, but they stopped where that little street opened onto the Old Town Square. Ludmilla pointed across the Square to the Gothic St Nicholas Church on the opposite side.

'Look,' she said. 'That's where Radio Prague transmitted from after their headquarters were bombed. Now it looks so beautiful, with those twin spires. That copper cladding makes a wonderful contrast to the stonework.'

All was quiet, but they remained in the small street, looking across to the Old Town Hall. The afternoon sun had mellowed its stones so that they glowed with a honey colour. The globes atop the tower's spires shone gold, and the tower itself threw a long shadow into the ancient Square.

'It is lovely, isn't it?' murmured Ludmilla, taking in the remarkable Orloj, the Astronomical Clock set into the lower part of the Town Hall's tower.

'It's a masterpiece of ingenuity,' Alex marvelled, 'and to think it was installed in 1410. It's not only a clock, but it reveals the date, and shows the positions of the Sun, the Moon, Earth, and even the zodiac constellations.' He shook his head in admiration.

'It's a pity it isn't operating fully, otherwise we could see the procession of the saints on the hour, but just taking in that incredible dial is wonderful.' He turned to Ludmilla. 'I was thinking of Blažena and her little boy.' He took Ludmilla's hand. 'Maybe it's the right time to think of getting married and starting a family ourselves.'

Ludmilla stared at him. 'Why now?'

'Well,' Alex looked very serious. 'We've known each other for a long time now, and hopefully, the war is almost over. We've both been through really difficult times—you suffering the loss of your people at Lidice, and me being constantly harassed by the Gestapo in my job, not knowing if I was going to be hauled away to prison at any moment. Maybe we can make a start on our new life.' He looked a little embarrassed.

Ludmilla reached up and kissed him. 'You old softie—is this a proposal?'

'Yes, it is, even if it's an awkward one,' Alex grinned. 'What do you say?'

'I think it's been a long time coming, but yes, I accept. Let's do it.' She looked across to the Old Square. The sun's dying rays shone on the Orloj's gilded face, creating something magical. 'Maybe we can get married in the Old Town Hall, if they still have a registry office there.'

Alex took her hand. 'That would be wonderful,' he agreed.

They walked hand in hand back to the apartment, as dusk settled over the city. The lengthening shadows seemed less threatening than before, and they wove their plans with an optimism neither of them had felt earlier.

* * *

They heard the news a couple of days later. A Nazi armoured vehicle was making a last-ditch effort to flush out resistance fighters thought to be hiding in the catacombs beneath the Old Town Square. Thinking that more fighters were in the Town Hall's tower, they opened fire with anti-aircraft guns. The Town Hall and other buildings were damaged. Worse, the sculptures on either side of the beautiful Orloj were burned, and the calendar dial face of the Orloj was badly damaged. Prague's most famous landmark was a smoking ruin.

Ludmilla wept when she heard the reports. 'Why did they have to destroy that?' she sobbed. 'Of all the buildings in the city, why that?'

Alex tried to comfort her, helpless in the face of her distress. He took her hands in both of his. 'I know,' he said gently, 'but at least we have the memory of seeing it in all its beauty on our special night.'

He held Ludmilla in his arms. 'We must remember it as it was before they attacked it,' he consoled her, 'and we have the memory of the lovely Saint Nicholas Church. We can be grateful that it was spared any damage.'

Ludmilla sighed. 'Yes—I suppose we must be grateful for something.'

The day after the attack on the Old Town Hall, the Germans left Prague as the victorious Soviet army rolled in on the ninth of May. Five years of German oppression dissipated, to be gradually replaced by the Soviet presence and a very uncertain future.

CHAPTER TWENTY-FOUR

The initial response to the Soviet presence was one of elation. Five years earlier, German armoured cars and tank treads had punished Prague's ancient cobblestones, and citizens had hurled insults and stones at the invaders. Prague's people had endured physical hardships due to the scarcity of food and clothing. Their cultivated lifestyle had been replaced by the terrors of occupation. Many had died or just simply disappeared under the Nazi repression.

Initially, after the Nazi defeat, it was as if an iron mesh had been lifted, and people felt they could look up and breathe freely. The absence of German military vehicles grinding along the streets was an enormous relief, as was discovering public ways now free of Gestapo and SS agents.

Now, in an ironic turnaround of sentiment, women and children passed up flowers to smiling Russian soldiers on their tanks and vehicles. Some of the Russians were playing their accordions as they moved through the streets. Russian soldiers passed out small Russian flags, and people in the crowds waved them along with the Czech flags, creating little seas of fluttering red, white and blue—a colourful melding of cultures, which added to the atmosphere of gaiety.

Some Czechs felt much less festive though, acutely aware of soldiers anywhere, and especially of these young, victorious Russian ones. To avoid any untoward encounters, young daughters were hastily secreted away in any number of safe hiding places from the notice of lustful eyes.

Many Czechs regained their properties in the Sudetenland when Germans either fled or were evicted. Occasionally, they would find holes in their yards or broken bricks in walls where the evicted Germans had returned during the night to dig up or extract valuables they had hidden.

'The Germans treated us badly when they were in power,' Alex remarked, 'and now the situation is reversed. This is what war does to people.'

* * *

A week later, Alex had news when he came home. 'President Beneš is back,' he announced, 'all the way from government-in-exile in England!'

Ludmilla looked up from her sewing. 'And did he bring his wife with him?'

'Oh, yes,' Alex curled his lip. 'He brought Hana. And from the newspaper reports, we are to assume that he alone is responsible for the fact that Prague suffered such little damage during the war, because he conceded so long ago in Munich by resigning.'

Alex shrugged. 'After all, he is a politician, and they always like to cover themselves with glory. Although,' he conceded, 'the Czech government was the only Eastern European exile government allowed to return home.'

Ludmilla put her work down. 'We seem to be living in some kind of vacuum, don't we? The Germans are gone, the Soviets are still here, and now we have a Czech government of a sort. Do you think the Soviets will stay?'

'I think there's a good chance they may.' Alex looked gloomy. 'After all, if you remember from that agreement made in Yalta back in February, we are seen to be in the Soviet sphere. We just have to wait and see. After all, we do have our own home-grown socialism in the form of the Czech Communist Party.'

Alex frowned. 'I really feel that the Third Republic is only a compromise, and very fragile. It's highly likely that the Czech Communist Party will win out. Time will tell.'

His expression lightened. 'Still, life is starting to pick up again. Businesses are re-opening. There's much more activity, and at least we can see a little more food appearing in the markets.'

'Maybe,' Ludmilla agreed, 'but we still have to queue a lot for supplies as we did during the war, and when we get to the serving counter, the choice is rather poor. Let's hope that the food situation improves with time.'

'Well, after all this time, we seem to be returning to something like normality, but'—here Alex's face wore the shadow of doubt—'it's nothing like before, and who knows just how long it will take?'

* * *

Blažena had just stepped from her house into the street on her way to do some shopping when she found herself facing a sea of angry female faces, which seemed to appear out of nowhere. Some she knew to be her neighbours. Others were strange to her. Then the insults were hurled. A gobbet of phlegm directed by someone landed at her feet.

'Whore!' one shouted. 'Slut!' shrieked another. Some women were shaking their fists at her. Blažena recognised one woman as the curtain-twitcher from the house opposite.

'What—?' Blažena gasped, alarmed at their anger, which flowed across to her like a violent wave. 'Why are you—?'

'Don't play the innocent with us, Brodsková!' screeched Teresa Beranková, Miroslav's former neighbour.

'What have I done?' Blažena pleaded. 'Why are you all so angry?' Suddenly, fear constricted her heart. She was apprehensive, not only for herself but for Gizela and the children if they suddenly returned and became embroiled in the altercation, which, judging by the almost tangible mood of aggression radiating at her, could intensify dangerously.

Tereza Beranková strode forward, arms on her hips. 'You know very well what you've done, and brought shame on all the women of Rakovník!' She shook a fist at Blažena, her eyes blazing. 'You consorted with that German, the one we all saw coming to your house, and you all dressed up like a prostitute driving away in that great car of his to do Heaven knows what!' Her face was scarlet with fury.

Blažena glanced over their angry faces at the two bearded warriors frozen in conflict on the sgraffito façade opposite. *Why are people always fighting?* She shook her head in despair. 'Tereza, you of all people should know me better than that! You were my father's friend. I've never hurt anyone. You must know I was forced to go to their horrible receptions. What would have happened if I had refused? To me? To my little children? Can't you understand the precarious situation I was in?' Now Blažena was seething at their unjust accusations. 'And what about the other people in Rakovník who also had to attend the Nazis' functions? What are you planning for them?'

Mutinous, Beranková continued to press her case. 'All I know is what I've seen with my own eyes. It's not about them—it's about you, coming and going, prostituting yourself, and you know what happens to women who have been collaborating with the enemy? They get their hair shorn, and then they're paraded around the town square!' She challenged Blažena, chin up, triumphant.

A shaking Blažena drew breath in order to defend herself, when a lone voice was raised from the far side of the crowd. 'Are you mad? Have you all forgotten? This lady is the one who tried to save the Goldmann's little boys when the Gestapo were going to take them away! She and her family could have been taken to a labour camp for that, or worse, shot!'

Blažena peered over to the far side of the crowd, to see Michaela Horáková, her shopping acquaintance. *Bless you, Michaela; you spoke up just in time.*

The fierce energy of the group dissipated as the women began arguing with each other, before silently disbanding. A red-faced Tereza Beranková slunk away. Blažena managed to beat a strategic retreat back up her front steps and into the house, where she slammed the door closed and collapsed into a chair, still shaking.

Then the tears started. Blažena wept for her own parents and Helena, Ludmilla and her lost family, Josef, the two little Goldmann boys, and even for Helmut von Neumann, swept away with the other Germans by the Soviets, like chaff before the wind. If the truth be told, she even wept a little for herself.

It was some time before she was able to collect herself and consider from the morning's confrontation just how easily a group's anger could be whipped up. She could well understand how a country's attitude could be swayed by a master manipulator like Goebbels.

* * *

Young Slava needed care, so it was difficult for Blažena to leave home for prolonged periods of time. Gizela could not be expected to take more responsibility than she already had. Film production in Prague had slowed considerably, so Radek had more time to come to Rakovník.

'Things are very slow on the Hill,' he remarked conversationally, 'the good thing is that Barrandov now has those three new sound stages nearing completion—the so-called "New Halls" that Goebbels had constructed. That means Barrandov now has the potential to be a great centre for film production.' He sighed. 'Still, I grieve for the loss of Pragcine. In a way, it was my child.'

'I know,' Blažena sympathised, and she put her hand over his. 'But we did some wonderful work then, didn't we?'

Radek smiled. 'True, true,' he admitted. 'But I don't think any of it would have happened if I hadn't met my cloud dreamer.'

Blažena remembered their first encounter very well, and smiled at the recollection. Then she brought the conversation around to the present. 'Who will be producing now?' she queried. 'The Germans took Barrandov Studios from Miloš Havel, and then his AB Corporation was renamed Deutsche Prag-Film. Who owns it now?'

'Well, we know that last year some communist elements wanted Barrandov nationalised, and it was approved in principle by the Czech government-in-exile. We've yet to learn what happens there.' Radek shrugged. 'Whatever happens, I know that Pragcine is gone for good, and it's anyone's guess what will happen to the other studios on the Hill. Hopefully, production might resume slowly, provided there are enough technical people who survived the war. Some actors and actresses have either left for other countries, died or been killed.'

Blažena was despondent. 'Are there so many who are not available now?'

'Well, the Nazis were very efficient at eliminating those who resisted their will, as we know. And, it's to our detriment, because it meant so much wasted talent.' Radek shook his head. One thing's for sure—Miloš Havel's situation is very precarious.'

CHAPTER TWENTY-FIVE

It was 1948. 'Well,' Radek addressed the group assembled in the former Pragcine's city office, 'it's been a long three years since the Germans were defeated. We've had this interminable period of inertia. So many talented people in our industry left the country just before the war. A few of our good directors continued to make films, against various obstacles. Some, unhappily, were murdered by the Nazis. The writer and director Jan Sviták was murdered at the end of the war by an anti-fascist group.'

'And we all remember Lida Baarová, and the scandal she caused by being Goebbels' mistress. Well, Hitler blocked that and prevented her from leaving Germany, even though she wanted to go to Hollywood. She thought she could become another Marlena Dietrich!'

Heads turned to see who the speaker was. Of course, it was the irrepressible cameraman Stefan, who always had an ear for gossip.

'Yes,' Stefan went on, 'near the end of the war, she was in Italy and tried to escape back to Germany, but was extradited to Czechoslovakia. Then she was in custody for collaboration. Her poor mother died, and her sister committed suicide. All over a love affair with Goebbels!'

Stefan's assistant Ondřej was sitting next to him. 'Well, Dietrich was much smarter than Baarová,' he remarked. 'Even though Hitler was a great fan of hers, she managed to become an American citizen at the start of the war. She worked for the Allies all over the place, even coming to Germany with General Patton. Hitler wanted her to come back to Germany permanently, but she was too smart to do that!'

Several heads nodded, and there were mutterings in the audience.

'These stories are all very entertaining, but we're no further ahead, are we?' someone interjected impatiently.

'That's so correct,' Radek conceded. 'A lot of political in-fighting has been going on, and due to the strength of the communist element in the government, President Beneš has capitulated. Now we are under President Klement Gottwald's Government, which in effect means Soviet rule.' Radek looked grim. 'As we know, President Gottwald is a strong supporter of Joseph Stalin. Take that as you will.'

'What does that mean for Barrandov, and everyone working there?' someone else demanded.

Radek shrugged. 'You all know we lost Pragcine when the Nazis took over, and Barrandov became Deutsche Prag-Film. You also should know that some in the Communist Party had requested during the war that Barrandov be nationalised. The request was sent to the then government-in-exile in London.' He sighed. 'Unhappily, the request was approved so in all but name, we have been nationalised since 1945. Soon, Barrandov Studios will cease to exist and it will become Czechoslovak State Film, operating under Soviet censorship.'

'I know.' Radek raised his hands against a groundswell of questions and protests. 'The situation for us is uncertain. Possibly the best option is that we will be permitted to function, but under a different kind of censorship. And,' he added, 'it's almost certain that the freedom of subjects for films will be constricted. But'—he raised his hands for emphasis— 'we should feel a bit optimistic, because some companies are gearing up to start filming. We can only wait and see.'

Everything old is new again. Blažena sighed. *Under the Nazi régime, I made films under their censorship, and this will be no different. It's just another set of ideological constraints.*

When everyone else had wandered out, voices raised in comment and complaint, Blažena stayed behind. Radek remained at his desk, head in hands—the picture of defeat.

'Does this mean it's over?' Blažena queried, 'all those years of hard work you and everyone has put in?'

Radek raised his head. His bright blue eyes met hers. 'I honestly don't know. I sincerely hope not. No doubt a committee or committees will be set up, as is always the case with this kind of régime, and then directives will filter down to us mere mortals.' He reflected a moment. 'Of course, if the directives are intelligent, it might mean that we can continue to make films as before. After all, the Russians have a fine history of film-making, especially in film technique and theory.'

Radek's eyes took on a faraway look. 'I can remember seeing the films of Sergei Eisenstein.' He smiled at the thought of himself as a young man soaking up motion film. 'Eisenstein was such a rev- olutionary, you know, and when he combined his ideological ideas to his concept of editing, of montage, the effect was electrifying.'

'Well, if the Russians have a tradition of cinema, that sounds a little positive,' Blažena ventured, 'maybe the future won't be so bleak.'

Radek's smile was sardonic. 'Well, just remember the Russian Revolution and the chaos that ensued after it. Maybe they'll accept our style of cinema, or maybe our creativity will be crushed like a beetle!'

'That would be an enormous pity,' Blažena com- miserated, 'especially now that Barrandov has those three nice sound studios that Goebbels kindly had constructed. It would be a great shame not to take advantage of them.'

Radek agreed. 'We just have to wait and see just what conditions will be imposed on film-making at Barrandov, because, as night follows day, there will be conditions.'

* * *

'I want to discuss something with you,' Radek said when Blažena and he were having coffee in Kavarna Slavia. Blažena had been living quietly at home in Rakovník for a few years, but now that Slava was nearly five years old, felt she could visit Prague to reconnect with Radek and the film business. After all, Zdenek was able to come home for weeks at a time until his next engagement, and this freed her.

Radek leant forward confidentially. 'The Soviet censors are very watchful. Some films are being made, but they seem to be around very safe material— nothing provocative. I think we could venture a new film next year, as long as it doesn't offend the powers that be.'

Blažena brightened. 'Might there be a part for me? I know I'm no longer the ingenue, but I'm only in my thirties.'

'Oh, I think I can find a part for you,' Radek smiled. 'Our working title is *The Wild Girl*, and it deals with a recluse who is skilled at making up natural remedies.'

Blažena looked offended. 'Does that mean that I'm a witch?' She snorted.

'No—not at all,' Radek was reassuring. 'She's generally liked by the people whom she helps, but there are others who regard her with great suspicion. There's a scene where ignorant people storm her house with pitchforks, but it's all resolved in the end.' He grinned. 'You see, we have to be careful, too. It's a morality tale, and the moral is, you shouldn't judge a book by its cover.'

* * *

Blažena was intrigued by this very different role and film, and spent some time at Barrandov, watching at a respectful distance in the backlot—the large area for outside scenes— as skilled carpenters and artists created a humble cottage surrounded by groves of trees and undergrowth which gave the impression of a forest. It was a miracle of illusion, especially the cluster of houses which were to serve as the village for the tale. From one side they looked extremely real, but from the other side—nothing but plain wood and timber supports.

'Hello! What are you doing here?' Radek's familiar voice startled her out of her contemplation of the sets.

Blažena smiled. 'I was just thinking how different this film will be,' she said. 'Some of my earlier characters were dreamers.' She frowned. 'Of course, those films I had to do for Goebbels were propaganda, based on the model of an Aryan perfection, but my character here has to fight not only for her reputation but possibly also her life.' She turned to face Radek. 'It's a new direction, and a bit of a challenge.'

Radek looked concerned. 'Are you worrying about it?'

Blažena laughed. 'Oh, no. I'm always up for a challenge!' She turned to view the set under construction, but fingered her precious locket all the same.

* * *

Radek's prediction on the nature of films to be produced during the next few years proved to be correct. Under the vigilant eye of the Soviet censor, politically non-threatening films were produced. Several of these were fables, some based on the classics, and they brought light-hearted relief from the harrowing years of conflict.

One of these was *The Proud Princess*, which proved to be the most viewed Czech film ever. Some years later, the film adaption of Jaroslav Hašek's famous *The Good Soldier Švejk* drew on a literary theme, and proved very popular. Radek's own film *The Wild Girl* was very popular, too.

'It was a very different film,' Blažena commented to Radek, 'an apparent fable, but with strong moral values.'

Radek nodded. 'Given the actions of the Communist Party, everyone is frightened. You know, thousands lost their jobs, lots of people were arrested and tortured, and thousands fled the country, so everyone is treading very carefully.'

'I heard that Miloš Havel is having serious problems,' Blažena commented.

'Problems is an understatement,' Radek shrugged. 'He lost everything at Barrandov, and tried to emigrate, but his visa was denied. Then he was put on trial for collaboration with the Nazis.' Radek's smile was grim 'He was cleared, but banned from film-making forever. He tried to leave again, but was thrown into jail.'

Blažena was horrified. 'After all he did for the film industry, that's terrible!' she exclaimed.

'Yes, it is,' Radek agreed, 'but he was released due to poor health and is staying with the Havel family. It's a great shame that a giant of the Czech film industry has been brought so low. His future looks bleak.'

CHAPTER TWENTY-SIX

'Well, we still don't know where we are.' Radek was gloomy. He and Blažena were in an office at Barrandov Studios. 'Since Barrandov has become Czechoslovak State Film, everything comes down from a series of committees. This means that very little gets done in reality.'

Blažena commiserated. 'I know. I even had a visit at my Prague apartment by two gloomy Party members asking about the number of bedrooms I had. I explained that I had to use the apartment in Prague when I was working on films, but they didn't seem impressed at all. I have the feeling that the Party is just sniffing around for extra living space. I have the feeling that they are suspicious of the arts in any of its forms.

'They even warned that I might expect to have strangers living in my apartment! I've heard the same thing in Rakovník. They say it's about better housing for all, not just the privileged. Why on earth should they have to do that?' She drew breath. 'And, apparently, teachers are asking their classes to comment on conversations or parties their parents are having, and to report anything said against the Party!' *My Slava is only five, and he would do anything his teachers told him. He would be a good little Pioneer, or whatever they call those children's groups.*

Blažena frowned. 'I'm a little concerned about Slava, I must confess. Apparently, schools are encouraging their students to go on so-called "civic exercises", which means going to farms to dig potatoes, or clean streets, or suchlike. They're given little booklets, and if they perform well, they get stars in them. They're just being brainwashed!'

Radek raised his eyebrows in surprise. 'I'm not surprised that you're concerned—it's just turning them into good little communists!'

He looked a little pleased. 'I've no idea about that, but the powers that be shouldn't be suspicious of this next film that we're proposing, anyway. We have to collaborate with one or two other companies to propose it,' said Radek.

Blažena brightened. 'What do you have in mind?' She queried. 'Might there be a part for me?'

Radek looked sombre. 'Well, the film isn't at all offensive. The Party should even like the theme. It's about the battle between the diminished German forces and the Prague people. It's urban anti-Nazi propaganda, if you like. The working title is *Silent Barricade.*'

Blažena was instantly alert. 'That means it's about the Prague uprising, isn't it? Well, there should be no issues there, since the Soviet troops came in at around the same time, and for exactly the same reasons.'

'I know, but there's something strange about the discussions so far.' Radek shook his head in frustration. 'I don't know what they're planning and apparently, I can co-direct, but without a screen credit. They're considering you for a major part, but you might not get any credit, either.'

Blažena was dismayed. 'Why would they do that?' she demanded. 'I'm not a political animal!'

'I understand that,' Radek commiserated, 'but you were in those two pro-German films made for Goebbels.'

Blažena was so angry that her complexion changed colour. 'They should know that there was no option! I had to comply, otherwise I possibly could have been thrown into prison or even shot! You understand that, surely!'

'I do, I do,' Radek admitted, 'and I told them exactly that. But the Soviets seem to think like dinosaurs, and can't understand anything except their own ideology. Not giving you a screen credit is some kind of punishment in their eyes, I think. Or, they might just be suspicious of our political leanings.' But then his eyes twinkled. 'Even if you might be anonymous, our make-up department can work it so you would be recognised immediately. Sometimes it's better just to go with their dictate.'

* * *

The meeting, when it occurred, was unlike any she had participated in. Now she and Radek, along with the other short-listed actors, had to confront a committee of dour-faced Party officials. The latter talked among themselves, resulting in those on the other side of the table shifting about nervously. Finally, the leading official gave the committee's judgement. As Radek had predicted, he would be permitted to co-direct. Blažena would have a role, but would not receive a screen credit.

Blažena raised her head, and would have spoken, but caught a warning look from Radek. 'Just leave it,' he whispered. 'You can't do anything.'

The meeting adjourned, and they prepared to leave, when Radek was called aside. Blažena waited outside in a flurry of anxiety. Finally, he appeared. When they were alone, Blažena couldn't contain her curiosity.

'What on earth did they want with you?' she asked.

Radek was gloomy. 'They offered me an ultimatum,' he said. 'Apparently, the Party approves of the films

I have made—they said they even liked them, which was a compliment of sorts, I guess—and want me to continue at Czechoslovak State Film. But'—he raised his hand to stop Blažena's excitement—'there's a condition. I must join the Party to guarantee any more work.'

Later, in their shared refuge of Kavarna Slavia, Radek and Blažena discussed the ultimatum.

'This the only work I know,' Radek confessed. 'I've done nothing else, and at my age, I wouldn't know where to start, especially now that the Party can allocate any kind of work to anyone.'

Blažena considered. 'Well, I love acting, and it's my only line of work, too,' she said. 'But at least I have Zdenek, who's earning an income. I wouldn't know what to say if they asked. Maybe it won't come to that.'

'Well,' Radek consoled her, 'at least we can look forward to working on *Silent Barricade*.'

* * *

Blažena was moved by working on *Silent Barricade*. The film was based on real events, in which citizens joined together to deter a German tank brigade heading for the city by blocking roads with diverted tram cars, and building barricades from bricks and rubbish at strategic intersections.

During filming, some shoots were done on locations in familiar parts of the city, especially Bartolomějská

Street, where partisans had commandeered AMR 35 tanks to fight the incoming Germans.

Bartolomějská was Ludmilla's street, and the reenactment of recent history resonated strongly with Blažena. While she was working in those scenes, she felt intensely proud that ordinary people had the courage to resist the invaders.

After filming, Blažena faced another meeting with a couple of party officials.

'Comrade Brodsková, can you tell us how you perceived the theme of *Silent Barricade*, and how you regarded your role in the film?'

Blažena was nonplussed. She had felt privileged to act in the film, and phrased her reply carefully.

'I saw *Silent Barricade* as being symbolic of the Czech people's determination to fight aggression. As for my participation, I saw my character as an ordinary person inspired by other ordinary people to attempt something extraordinary.'

'Comrade, you must be aware that you are a prominent actress. You are well known. Given your profile, we feel that you would be a definite asset if you joined the Party. We invite you to do so, and advise you to think carefully about this invitation. The interview is ended.'

Blažena rose from her chair, nodded to each of the officials, and managed to exit the room without revealing her emotions. She was shocked. She had not thought about joining the Party. Why would she? Blažena hurriedly sought out Radek, and they agreed to meet once more at Kavarna Slavia.

'I've been thinking about it seriously,' Radek said, 'and if I want to work anywhere in film, I have to join the Party. I lost Pragcine when the Germans took control. I know I won't ever regain a small production company under this régime. At least I can continue working if I sign to join the Party.' He sighed. 'I really love what I do, and I don't want to lose that.' He looked pleadingly at Blažena. 'Maybe it's a betrayal, but it's also survival.'

Blažena put her hand on his. 'I know, and I understand. I must make my own decision on this. I feel the same as you do. Acting has been my whole life. But—' She made an expression of disgust. 'I have real problems with their so-called invitation.'

* * *

Blažena was called to the Czechoslovak State Film offices the next day. She had agonised over the situation and was prepared for the interview.

'Well, Comrade Brodsková,' the surly senior agent said, 'Have you considered the Party's invitation?'

Blažena straightened her shoulders. 'Yes, Comrade,' she replied, 'I have, and my decision is that I do not wish to join the Party.'

'Comrade Brodsková, you have made your decision.' The senior interrogator's lips narrowed to a thin line. 'We will now make ours. You could have been a prominent advocate for the State, but since you do not wish to join the glorious Czechoslovak Communist Party, you will not be given any more roles, regardless of your eminent success. Should you rethink what we regard as an unfortunate choice, you may request another meeting. That is all. Thank you.'

Blažena bowed her head. 'As you wish,' she murmured. She felt numb in mind and body as she rose from her chair, determined not to betray any emotion, and walked from the room. Outside the door, she found a chair and collapsed onto it. She clutched her locket and tried to breathe normally. She had spent so much time and energy perfecting the skills that had led to her prominence as an actress. But now, her acting career, the profession which had given her so much joy and fame, was over.

CHAPTER TWENTY-SEVEN

Blažena lost no time in contacting Radek, asking to meet him in her Prague apartment. He arrived at their agreed time, and knocked on her door.

'Radek! Thank you for coming so promptly.' Gizela and the children were out, and Blažena was looking very miserable.

Radek was perplexed. 'Anything for you, Blažena,' he replied, 'but you look extremely upset. What on earth's the matter?'

Blažena tried to maintain her composure. 'I felt I should contact you first. After all, you are my trusted friend.'

'Always, my dear,' he responded, 'but please tell me what the problem is. You look terribly stressed.'

Blažena took a deep breath. 'The committee at the studios interviewed me again, and demanded I make a decision about their ultimatum.' She paused, her eyes brimming over with tears. 'Radek, I felt I couldn't agree to join the Communist Party. It's against all my feelings about freedom of speech and democracy!'

She clasped her hands together to prevent them from shaking. 'When I declined to join, they said that I can never work in films again. My career is over!'

Radek looked shocked. 'Why did you say that? You could have agreed, and acted as if it was a good thing.' He raised his voice. 'After all, you are a damned actress! Couldn't you just have played that part? Just given them lip service?'

'No-one would know, and you would still have your career and'—Radek was close to shouting now—'it would be a career enhanced because you would have become a prominent Party member!'

Blažena raised her hands in supplication. 'Don't hate me! I just couldn't do it. I can't live a lie!'

'Of course I don't hate you,' Radek sympathised, 'and I understand you had to obey your conscience, but you've just sacrificed your career unless you go crawling back to them, which I doubt very much. And—I'll miss working with you terribly.' He paused. 'Since we're into confessions, I have to admit that I've agreed to join their wretched Party. I love the work, and I need to earn an income. It's as simple as that.' He gave a twisted grin. 'Now I'm the actor, because I have to toe the Party line and pretend to agree to everything they say. We're both victims of the system now!'

* * *

When Radek had left, Blažena contacted Ludmilla. 'Could you come around to the apartment? I really need a sympathetic ear.'

'Fine—I can be there after work, and you can make me a coffee.' Ludmilla had regained a position of sorts in a very changed government. As she had said on more than one occasion, 'Here today, gone tomorrow.'

While Blažena waited in the lounge room, she gazed out at the sea of red tiled rooftops on adjacent buildings. She loved this apartment, this room, and could still see tiny Zdenka playing on the carpet, building with her coloured blocks. *My life here was full of promise. Our child grew here. We all anguished about the early signs of war here.* She closed her eyes. *Josef left here for another opera adventure, and never returned.* She sighed deeply. *It's not good to dwell too much on the past,* she told herself sternly, *but it's so difficult to forget it.*

When Ludmilla arrived, they embraced and went into the sitting room. Ludmilla relaxed while Blažena made coffee. She busied herself in the kitchen, grinding the beans and filling the coffee-pot. When the aromatic brew was done, she returned with coffee and cups on a tray, and sat down. She took a deep breath and recounted her experiences with the committee at the film studios, and their reaction to her refusal to join the Party.

Ludmilla was horrified. 'Does this mean that you can never work again?'

'Apparently, although I suppose if I "repent"'—she made air quotes for emphasis—'they might consider taking me back.' She squared her shoulders. 'But I think that's highly unlikely, given how I feel.' She looked down at the carpet, her hands locked together. 'I'm not as young as I was, and I don't know how many parts might come my way, but it's a wrench to lose the possibility.' She sighed. 'Working was so exciting! I loved the characters I created, the atmosphere in the sound studios—all of it.' She squared her shoulders again, then tried to relax them. 'Radek said that he's agreed to join the Party because he needs the work, and I can't blame him.'

Ludmilla was sympathetic. 'It's a very hard choice to make, but you've made it.' She took Blažena's hands. 'On a positive note, you've earned a nice amount from your films, and Zdenek is still working.'

'Yes, you're right, of course,' Blažena attempted a smile. 'I can accept the change, I suppose. I can devote more time to the children and Zdenek. Now—' She patted Ludmilla's hand. 'How are things with you and Alex? It's a while since I've seen you both.'

'Well,' Ludmilla tried to keep her expression neutral, but a wide smile broke out. 'Alex and I are expecting!' She shook her head in wonderment. 'I'll be an older mother, but hopefully, we will be a family!'

Blažena was delighted. 'I suppose Alex is thrilled.'

Ludmilla nodded. 'Of course he is, but here's the strange thing.' Her expression was serious. 'You wouldn't believe it, but this government is actually turning their attention to Lidice, as it was a German atrocity. I gave them all my family's details, and they're trying to trace survivors. If there are any, they would be nieces or nephews.' She attempted a smile, but her mouth quivered. 'It would be wonderful if we both had any remaining family from Lidice. It would be a miracle, really, because only around two dozen children survived.'

Blažena stared into space for a while. 'They were terrible times, weren't they?' she murmured and continued, 'And now we're living in very uncertain times again.' She sighed. 'When will it ever end?'

* * *

Some months later, Zdenek was finishing up for the day at Krušovice, not so far from Rakovník, when the project manager came into the temporary mobile site office.

'Ah, Comrade Brodsky,' his manner was brusque, as usual. 'There you are.'

Zdenek turned around and smiled. 'Yes, Comrade, I'm just completing tomorrow's task list. The building project is on schedule, I'm happy to report.'

'Good, good,' his manager seemed slightly distracted. 'You do recall the conversation we had some time ago, about the advantages of joining the Party?'

Zdenek nodded. 'Yes, I recall we spoke about that, but I haven't come to a decision yet. I have been preoccupied with the success of the building project. Is it so important?'

His manager puffed out his chest. 'It's very important, Comrade! Everyone must work together for the glory of the Communist Party. Unfortunately, you don't seem to think that the Party and the State are important. Because of your way of thinking, I am demoting you from senior construction engineer to building supervisor, effective tomorrow.

You will provide your superior with all the details of your plans and figures for this project. If you reconsider your attitude, you can arrange to see me to discuss the matter.'

He turned on his heel and went out of the office, leaving a stunned Zdenek staring at the closed door.

* * *

'I'll be home more now,' Zdenek announced on his arrival home. He looked sober. 'You know how the communists like to punish people who have some qualifications by reversing their positions?' He sighed. 'Well, they've just redefined my position, and instead of being a senior construction engineer, I'm going to be demoted to an ordinary building supervisor. I don't think it matters whether I join their Party or not, it's just something they like to do, even if it makes no sense at all.' He attempted a laugh. 'It looks like you and I are in the same pickle, up to a point. We're both out of favour.'

He looked at Blažena, his expression serious. 'Oh, and another thing— I'll probably lose my small apartment here. The Party has this policy of improving housing for all, which means many people will either lose their property, or be forced to divide property and let strangers live with them. The rich are becoming the new poor, as they are losing their houses and being made to live in country areas.'

Blažena looked horrified. 'Does that mean I'll lose the Prague apartment? There was mention some time ago when those dreadful people came to inspect the rooms, but I thought the plans hadn't been formalised.'

Zdenek nodded. 'I think it's a distinct possibility that they have, but with the number of people living in this house, they might look the other way and let us stay. We're living in a strange new world, and who knows how everyone can cope with all the new regulations. We just have to survive.'

He smiled gently. 'I know it's a blow to lose your career, but you've worked for a long time, and really, you deserve to slow down.'

Blažena laughed ruefully. 'I know, and I'll accept it in time. I'll just become Blažena Brodsková, housewife.' She shrugged. 'Anyway, it's just another role. Life will be more relaxed, and I can be a better wife and mother, instead of living dreams.'

Blažena tried to reconcile her decision and her future without life in filming, but once or twice she wandered into the bedroom and opened the large wardrobe where her costumes were hanging. She would run her hands over them, and take them out one by one. *You're from Escape from Darkness. And, oh, I wore you in Enduring Love.* She would always hastily return another. *That was for Wounded Heart. I can't bear that one now. That's when Josef disappeared.* She would go through them all in turn, speaking to them as if they were animate. Then she would give a deep sigh, bow her head, close the wardrobe door gently, and go out.

CHAPTER TWENTY-EIGHT

Blažena was on one of her grocery shopping expeditions, which were becoming very frustrating due to the scarcity of anything worthwhile to buy, when she noticed some activity near the square. She abandoned her shopping quest, which involved having to wait in a long queue to purchase a kilogram of dubious-looking potatoes in order to buy two hundred and fifty grams of inferior meat. Everyone endured this, since any complaint or signing of petitions brought swift reprisal, even to the extent of imprisonment by Party officials.

A truck was parked near the Town Hall, and men in overalls were busy setting up a ladder, cables and odd horn-shaped objects. Blažena was fascinated. 'What is it?' she asked a man standing close by.

He frowned. 'I hear it's going to be our new radio system.'

In her usual fashion, Blažena was inquisitive. 'How can it be? You need a radio station and a transmitter for that, surely.'

Her companion laughed. 'Not in our glorious Soviet system. Information and instructions are going to come by wire from inside the Town Hall. Those horns are speakers, so we can't help but hear what they say!'

* * *

Blažena mentioned it to Zdenek when he came home. 'Oh, they're going up everywhere,' he said with a curl to his lip. 'Our Party is going to make sure everyone gets their message, like it or not.'

It was just as Zdenek said. Soon horns were installed in every street, braying their propaganda and instructions via powerful amplifier systems in the Town Hall. No-one dared complain, because the gossip would be carried by devotees of the Party, and recriminations would follow.

Blažena was disturbed at home one day when two burly men in overalls knocked on her door. They were carrying a large grey box with cabling attached.

'Who are you?' she demanded. 'What do you want?'

One of the men displayed his Party badge. Blažena recognised the Czech flag above the Soviet hammer and sickle. 'We have instructions to install your new radio, Comrade Brodsková. All houses and shops will have them.' The other workman was scanning a suitable wall for mounting.

'But,' a mutinous Blažena objected, 'I already have a good radio, and it's working perfectly.'

The man's companion grinned. He had a couple of teeth missing, making him look slightly sinister. 'It might be working perfectly now, Comrade, but soon you won't be able to receive some stations, especially those capitalist ones from other countries. Listening to them will be against Party rules. This box is Radio by Wire, and it will play nice programs, including the Party news service. You can turn the sound up or down, but it will only be the one station.'

Blažena looked in consternation at her own excellent radio. It was a Rel Signal, a handsome model in a large wooden cabinet with a beautiful veneer finish. It even had a neon indicator to enable accurate tuning. It was her pride and joy. 'You're not going to take it away, are you?' she pleaded.

'Oh, no,' one of the men smirked, 'You'll just find you can't listen to forbidden stations. We have the technology to interfere with their signals. We call it "jamming".'

Later, when they had departed after mounting the ugly grey box up on a wall and connecting it to outside cabling, Blažena tried to listen on her own radio to one or two foreign stations that interested her. Two that she tried, Radio Free Europe and Radio Luxembourg, only emitted harsh static noise, and were impossible to understand. *So, this is how they are going to control our hearts and minds. Are we all going to become robots in thrall to the Communist Party?*

After she had failed to find the stations she wanted, she stood and glared up at the grey speaker mounted on the wall, as if it was personally responsible for her anger at the intrusion it represented.

'Well, if I don't want to, I don't have to listen to you, you wretched thing,' she muttered. The grey speaker, understandably, uttered no reply.

From then on, Blažena found that there were mixed reactions to the new Radio by Wire. Many people she either talked to or overheard in the town square were happy with the new arrangement, and Blažena enquired of those she knew why it was so.

'Well, I like it,' said Daniela Dušková, one acquaintance Blažena enjoyed having coffee with in the town square. 'It's because I couldn't afford to buy a radio receiver—they're so expensive, and very difficult to obtain.'

Blažena had a question. 'What do you think of the programs?'

'Well, they're better than nothing, which is what I had before!' Daniela laughed. 'Something is better than nothing, I always say.'

Some of Blažena's acquaintances had objected to the new speakers installed in their homes, because they found the concept intrusive. 'But,' as another of her friends reasoned, 'I didn't like the idea of having it in the house, but I can always turn the volume down!'

Even Blažena had to admit that this new service sometimes had its good points. For one thing, there were nice music programs, and also radio dramas, which she enjoyed immensely. *I really shouldn't like it*, she reasoned, *because I believe that it's subtle propaganda, and its drip-feed is designed to lull us into acceptance.*

* * *

'Radek! How nice to see you again!' Blažena was truly pleased to see him. Even though they no longer had any professional connection, they stayed in touch due to their strong bond of friendship. They embraced, Radek kissing her on each cheek.

'I have considerably more free time now.' He grimaced. 'Nothing is like it was, and I just have to wait to see if I get selected to do anything. Still,' he shrugged, 'it's better than nothing.'

'What's being planned?' Blažena was curious, even though she was no longer in the profession.

'Well, there's a very nice film coming up, based on a novel by Fráňa Šrámek.'

'Fráňa Šrámek? Wasn't he a bit of an anarchist? A poet, too?' Blažena recalled that Šrámek had the reputation of being politically incorrect.

'Yes, true,' said Radek, 'but this piece is *Silvery Wind*, and it's a very sweet rite of passage novel. It deals with a boy who learns about life and love through his relationships.' He paused. 'I'd really like to work on it, but direction is via the panel process as usual.'

Radek grinned. 'There's one really interesting actor who'll probably be cast—Miloš Forman. He's very talented, and I think he'll go on to do interesting things. I know Vaclav Krška is a contender for director, but we'll see.'

Blažena sighed and looked down at her hands, once so expressive in the profession she still could have pursued had she so decided. Then she looked up and smiled. 'All the excitement—I really miss it, but I'm still happy with myself for the decision I made.'

Radek smiled. 'I understand,' he said. 'But now, a little bit of gossip! You knew that Miloš Havel had managed to leave Czechoslovakia, using a false passport? Well, he got to Munich, and he's suing UFA GmbH, the German film production company, for taking control of his interests in Barrandov Studios when Goebbels was Minister of Propaganda! Knowing Miloš, he'll probably win!' Radek laughed. 'He always was a sly old fox.'

* * *

Blažena was climbing the steps to her front door when she encountered the postman. He gave her a grin, and rummaged busily through his satchel.

'Here you are,' he said cheerfully and extracted an extremely battered postcard, which he put into her hand. Blažena continued up the steps, and went inside. She sat down to examine the card. It was dated 1946, and posted in Berlin. It had been sent to the Prague apartment, and then redirected. She could barely make out the greeting. It was a plain message with the comment that the writer was enjoying life, and she could just make out the sender's name. Josef. That was it. There was no sender's address.

Blažena just sat there stunned, hand to her chest, clutching her locket with one hand while gripping the postcard with the other, as the blood pounded in her ears. She could barely breathe. *Where has Josef been all this time? What has he been doing? Is he still alive? Does this make me a bigamist?* When he had written it, he apparently had no desire to see her again—or did he? She felt a mix of grief and anger wash over her.

This was the nightmare of his disappearance playing all over again, like a dark mystery film. *What happened to him, and where has he been all this time?* Blažena was having difficulty digesting the meaning of the card. *Why didn't Josef return to me? I thought our love was forever!*

Her mind turned on the evening of their walk onto Charles bridge, with the beauty of Hradčany spearing a perfect sky sprinkled with stars, and the glittering river below. It had been a wonderful moment in her life. Blažena bent her head and a sob escaped her as she realised how ironic it was that she considered the stars surrounding the head of St John of Nepomuk as an omen.

Well, an omen, but obviously not a good one. How could he change and abandon me and his little child? This news from the past was devastating, and it was some time before she could breathe normally. The sense of loss overwhelmed her, and brought all the grief churning back. She wept a little. *My world has turned upside down again.* With a tremendous effort she composed herself, realising that the fates toyed with people as they chose, in some kind of terrible, incomprehensible game.

CHAPTER TWENTY-NINE

Blažena leant out from the front window seat of her sitting room, taking in the street and people walking up and down. She studied the sgraffito designs on the house opposite. It brought back vivid memories of the first time she walked through Prague with Ludmilla. She could even see in her mind's eye the beautiful Kafka house in the Old Town Square.

She sighed. This was so long ago, and she was now past middle age. *Did I really have a career in film?* From the idea of creating dreams in films, it seemed as if the memory was just a dream itself.

Her life now was like so many other people's— attempting to live under the claustrophobic atmosphere of communism. *It seems impossible that from an earlier carefree life, our country had suffered under the yoke of the German invasion.* Her mind went back again. *We enjoyed a brief period of hope and renewal, only to be subjugated once more.*

What was this new reality? The coercion of those who didn't comply with communism, and were interrogated, intimidated, and had their homes searched while the Secret Police invaded their privacy? To Blažena this was like living a nightmare—the worst kind of Kafkaesque scenario, where the presence of bugs in homes prevented their occupants from expressing anything but the most banal of conversations. And, for most of the time, this social invasion was merely an instrument of the new ideology—surreal, without sense or meaning.

Blažena shook her head slowly, as if to clear it from these fogging thoughts. *Why should Zdenek have been demoted just because he chose not to join the Party? He's a clever, talented engineer, capable of giving much to Czech society.*

Now, as a site building supervisor, Zdenek was creating paneláks—prefabricated apartment buildings which were constructed from the 1960s onwards. It was a government policy that all should have an equal standard of living. The result was tower block estates of apartments identical in every way, sprouting like giant mushrooms.

Everyone was expected to live in them, from factory workers to university professors. Blažena grimaced. *This is just another example of social levelling.* She pondered her husband. Zdenek was no longer young, and he would either voluntarily retire or maybe be forced to. *How will he feel? Thrown on the rubbish heap?* She chuckled to herself. *A bit like me, except I achieved that all by myself!*

She couldn't help another deep sigh. *Now tradesmen headed companies. Menial jobs like street sweeping or window washing were forced on those with higher qualifications.* To Blažena it was an inversion of social values. *I feel as if everyone is living in a giant vice, in which the vitality and happiness are being squeezed out of them, under a dark and gloomy cloud of social and political restraints.*

She shook her head to clear it, concerned that she was becoming maudlin. She wandered into the kitchen and, for something to do, made herself a cup of coffee and sat down at the table. It was so strange now to have no motivation, no excitement after those busy, creative years of film-making.

Only a few markers tied her to the new reality, and they were the lives of those around her— the people she liked and loved. Gizela, for one. Now middle-aged, she had gone back to Prague to care for her elderly mother. This had been a tremendous wrench for Blažena. Gizela had come to them young, with her blazing red hair, outlandish jewellery and tremendous vitality. *Zdenka loved her so much, and she was my right hand. But time passes, as she did.*

And Zdenka. A frown creased Blažena's forehead. Zdenka, now over thirty years old, had married, but

Blažena had wondered if she was ever really happy. Bohosh, Zdenka's husband, was pleasant enough, but at times was violent towards her. He travelled around communist countries as he had the dubious occupation of building crematoria—an odd profession, and rather a grim choice.

Shortly after their marriage, Bohosh had built a spacious, handsome villa and moved Zdenka into it. *They were happy for a while, but then something went wrong.* Bohosh began creating a lot of garden and cultivation space on the property and then, to Zdenka's horror, began to amass a menagerie of sheep, goats, rabbits and chickens.

He tried to make Zdenka a farmer's wife, but she had rebelled and refused to attend to the animals' needs. Blažena shook her head at the thought. *Bohosh should have realised Zdenka wasn't suitable for that lifestyle. She was too sophisticated.* Neighbours realised the situation and removed the animals to care for them, so she no longer had to play the country wife.

Blažena took another sip of her cooling coffee. *Then it all changed. I remember when the news came.* Bohosh's motorcycle had crashed, and he was dead. Zdenka was now a young widow with a child to support. What Zdenka didn't know was that he was actually riding to Prague to apply for a divorce as he had acquired a girlfriend, the fact of which Zdenka was sublimely unaware—even when the other woman showed up at the funeral.

Zdenka had remained in ignorance until the beautiful blonde in the large black hat broke down, sobbing uncontrollably. Zdenka was in two minds about whether to approach the beautiful stranger but initially, something held her back.

Eventually, she whispered to the grieving woman, 'I'm so sorry. Was he a relative of yours?'

The blonde turned, and with tears streaming down her face, she sobbed, 'He was my lover; my beautiful Bohosh, and now he's gone!'

Zdenka was speechless, and it was only through a near-miraculous effort at self-control, that she muttered something inconsequential and returned to her place. She had glared at the stranger, thinking the worst, wondering what probably had been taking place without her knowledge. Fortunately, Bohosh's divorce never went through, and Zdenka eventually inherited a property she never liked in the first place. *The fates at work again,* Blažena smiled thinly. *We can't ever escape them*

Then her mind passed to Slava, her youngest. He had been a beautiful child, but had shown signs of rebellion during adolescence. Blažena had agonised over his apparent eagerness to join one of the Brigades as a Pioneer. Zealous young people, they were willing to perform manual work in order to gain credits for the Party—and, Blažena assumed, also to be eager to carry any comments they thought subversive to their controllers. That had worried Blažena enormously, but fortunately he had passed through that minefield and now had settled down into maturity.

* * *

Radek and his colleagues were discussing the proposal for a new film in a suite of the Hotel Jalta when there was a sudden commotion outside. They all rushed over to the large window overlooking Wenceslas Square, to behold an amazing sight. By a rough count, hundreds of thousands of people were gathering in the Square below, filling it to the edges.

'They've all come to hear Alexander Dubček and Václav Havel,' someone said.

'That's remarkable.' Stefan, Radek's loyal cameraman, shook his head in disbelief. 'Who would have thought that Havel, a playwright who had been blacklisted and imprisoned by the communists, could become a political activist and a champion of democracy with his Charter 77 initiative?'

Radek nodded. 'It looks like it's become very popular, and Dubček always was a reformer, even though he was communist. Didn't he believe in his "socialism with a human face"?' He peered out of the window again. 'Most of them down there seem young, and a lot of those probably are students, but there are older people, too.'

Before their fascinated gaze, the numbers swelled, and the uniformed police and soldiers on the fringes of the crowd looked uneasy and reluctant to make a move. There had been some violence in the preceding days, and people had been shot. It looked as if the uniformed forces were reluctant to see any recurrence.

Then the unreal happened. People took their keys from their pockets and began jingling them. The sound grew and grew until the Square rang with a silvery clangour.

'It's a message! They're unlocking the barriers of communism!' Radek shouted. 'They're saying the communists are no longer welcome, and should go home!'

* * *

On a chilly November morning in 1989, Blažena answered the phone. It was an excited Radek.

'Blažena! You'll never guess what's happened!'

'Well, tell me.' Blažena had not long risen, and was enjoying a coffee. 'I'm not a mind-reader!'

Radek could hardly contain the excitement in his voice. 'It's over! communism is all over!'

'What? How?' Blažena was suddenly wide awake, coffee forgotten.

An excited Radek related the events in Wenceslas Square. 'It was a message,' he told Blažena. His voice thickened with emotion. 'There had been protests and demonstrations here in Prague for a while, mainly by students and young people. The jingling of the keys was a clear message that the communists were no longer welcome, and they should just go home. Miraculously, the communists did go, and now everyone wants Havel for President!'

Blažena's breath caught. 'But that's wonderful,' she enthused. 'Now, at last, our country is free.' Then her voice became solemn. 'Who could have thought,' she murmured. 'After all the upheaval to our lives, the grief, who could have thought it could end so peacefully?' She sighed. 'All that wasted time, and all our country's potential shackled by the irons of communism. And now it's all been swept away by the cleansing spirit of the people. There's hope for us all now.'

Blažena ended the call, and sat, sipping her now cold coffee, and reflected on what had just taken place. *It's become a new world, but not for me.* She put the cup down. Like the bitterness of the coffee, her thoughts held bitterness as well.

But the news was true. In the face of the people's solidarity, the communist Czech Government collapsed through what would come to be called the 'Velvet Revolution', and a new government, mainly composed of Havel's Charter 77 members, was appointed. Late in December, Havel became President. A new era had begun.

EPILOGUE

It was the following year. 'I don't know why we have to go to Prague,' Blažena grumbled. 'After all, I'm eighty years old and at my age, I'm comfortable just staying in my own home.' She looked mutinous, her blue-grey eyes sparking in defiance.

'You know why, Maminko,' Slava wheedled. 'Radek said it was important to see you.' Slava was trying to be both diplomatic and firm. 'And, you must know that the hairstyle that Elena did suits you very well.'

Elena, the stylist in question, had persuaded Blažena to try a new style that suited her. At the age of eighty, Blažena had retained her flawless complexion, and her dark blonde hair had faded only a little. Elena's suggestion of a tint had horrified her, but she had reluctantly given in when told how well it would suit.

'Ah, Radek,' Blažena had softened at the mention of his name. 'Dear Radek—I haven't seen him in quite a while, although we talk from time to time.' Her expression pensive, she murmured, 'We did some wonderful things in our time.' Then she added almost in a whisper, 'It was all so long ago.'

'Yes, and this is why you should make the effort to see him again, after all this time,' Slava was being very persuasive. 'And it won't be too much of an effort, you know. He's sending a car to pick us up.'

'But we will be so late getting back home,' Blažena protested. She was at the stage when any disturbance to her daily routine distressed her.

Slava hurriedly reassured her. 'But we don't have to come home late at night! Radek has arranged a stay at a good hotel in Prague, and we can come home tomorrow morning.'

Blažena, realising that she had been outmanoeuvred, yielded reluctantly, but fired one last salvo of her protest. 'You know, of course, that I have absolutely nothing to wear!' She glared in defiance.

'Maminko, of course you have something to wear,' Slava argued. 'You have all those stunning costumes from your films tucked away in your wardrobe.'

'Oh—' Blažena smiled wistfully at the thought. 'They were so lovely,' she mused. 'Created just for me, you know, for all those wonderful films.' She gazed into space, her expression gentle. 'It was all so long ago,' she murmured again.

Blažena had no need to worry about a dress—her figure had not changed one bit since her twenties, and years of training as an actress meant that she carried herself like a model. She inspected the costumes one by one. *Which one will be the best for tonight? The ball gown I wore in Wounded Heart? No—I couldn't bear to wear that one—it reminds me too much of losing Josef.* She opened another door. *Maybe the formal dress I wore in Enduring Love? Yes—that might do it.*

'Just pick one!' Slava called from the kitchen, where they had been sitting. 'You've got dozens!'

Yes, so many costumes, and so many characters. So much dreaming. So much of my life being someone else. Well, I've had plenty of time now to be just Blažena Brodsková.

'Are you close to finishing?' Slava was keeping an eye on the time. 'The car will be here soon.'

Blažena gave herself a final critical appraisal in the mirror. 'Yes, I'm all ready.' She came from her bedroom into the kitchen.

'Maminko, you look wonderful!' Slava's eyes shone with admiration and love. 'Radek might want you for another film yet!'

'No—those days are long gone,' she sighed, 'but they were heady days, and we created some wonderful dreams for people with our stories.'

* * *

The chauffeured car duly arrived, and they set off into an afternoon already closing in with shadows and a lowering sky, for it was late in the year. The car's headlamps speared tendrils of fog swirling in the dusk.

'I wonder where we might be staying tonight,' Blažena mused. 'Radek was rather mysterious.'

Slava hedged a little. 'He didn't say, but he's a very good organiser, as you would know from his directing!'

'True, true,' Blažena reflected. 'He smoothed the path for me in every film. We never put a step wrong. I'm glad he was still able to work, even if it meant joining that dreadful Communist Party. Now that's gone and our country is free again.' She smiled. 'It's as if a black cloud has lifted.'

Slava put his hand on hers. 'You did what you thought was right. Do you ever regret it?'

'Sometimes,' she admitted. 'But at least it brought me back into the real world with a vengeance!' She changed the subject. 'Will Zdenek be there?'

'If he can get away from work,' Slava said. 'He has to work long hours now.'

Blažena was quiet for the remainder of the journey. She was recalling the times she went back and forth from Rakovník to Prague—sometimes for work with Radek at Barrandov, while she used the Prague apartment, other times purely social to keep in touch with Ludmilla and Alex. She was happy they now had their beautiful daughter, who compensated Ludmilla for the terrible loss of her family at Lidice. *So much grief, so much happiness. Life seems to dole it out in equal measure.*

Past Malostranská, the Mánesův Bridge took them across the Vltava with a glimpse of the beautiful Rudolfinum, and then they were parallel to the river along Křižovnická and around Kavarna Slavia's corner into Národní.

Blažena's breath caught as she glimpsed the glowing lights of the café. It brought back so many memories of the times she and her friends had sought refuge from the world in its quiet elegance. She recalled when Ludmilla took her and Miroslav, on her first day in Prague. That had been an epiphany for her—the elegant lights and tables, and all those photographs of famous people on the walls. Her old world had morphed into a new, exciting one.

Then, in her mind's eye, she saw the dark vision of the German tanks grinding into the cobblestones outside the café when they invaded the city. *So many memories over so many years.* Unconsciously, she fingered her precious locket. It had travelled with her a long way.

In Národní, their driver slowed. 'I'll try to work my way into Vodičkova,' he said. 'That way, you won't have so far to walk.'

Blažena glanced curiously at Slava. 'Where on earth are we going?' she queried. 'I'm lost.'

Slava grinned. 'Don't worry, we're here.' He helped her from the car, and they looked at the building in front of them.

Blažena gasped. 'Oh—it's Lucerna Palace! I haven't been here for so many years. It was built by our President Havel's grandfather. Dear Miloš was the President's uncle, and Barrandov Studios was his brainchild. The main cinema was Bio Lucerna, I think. Miloš had a private little screening salon here.' She sighed. 'It's all in the past, now.'

They entered the famous Passage, with its brown-and-white chequerboard tile floor, the green marbled pillars and red arched windows rising up to an elegant domed ceiling.

Blažena grew querulous. 'I still don't understand why we're here,' she complained.

Slava gripped her hand. 'You'll soon find out,' he promised as he guided her up the grand staircase flanked by red marbled pillars, and into a large cinema. It had a raked floor, with elegant bracketed lamps in front of the boxes on either side, framed by curving arches.

'Oh,' breathed Blažena as she looked around her, and then there was Radek, still handsome, his hair now grey but his eyes sparkling brilliant blue as before. He moved forward to greet her.

'Dear Blažena,' he murmured, kissing her on both cheeks. 'It's wonderful to see you again.'

'I'll leave you with Radek,' said Slava. 'I'll see you later.'

'Now, Radek,' remonstrated Blažena, 'what's this all about? You didn't drag me all this way just to see a film!'

'No,' Radek answered, giving her his arm as they walked slowly down the central aisle. 'More than one.' In response to her startled look, he explained. 'When the communists took control of Barrandov, they didn't destroy the masters of all the films we made. They preserved them in the vaults, and they're in very good condition, even the colour ones. So now,' he grinned, 'knowing that you've had your eightieth birthday, we're showing all your films as a retrospective celebration of your career. You'll have to speak sometime during the week, but you can come back to Prague for that. I'll arrange everything. For now, though, we'll just relax for the opening screening.'

Blažena just stared at him, speechless, dimly aware that people in the audience were standing and applauding. Finally, they reached the seats reserved for them. Her mind still in a whirl, Blažena made out Zdenek, Zdenka, Slava and Gizela, and further along, Ludmilla and Alex.

The house lights dimmed, and the beautiful bronze-coloured curtains slowly opened. Through tear-filled eyes, Blažena made out her other, younger self, flickering up on the screen. 'Oh'—she breathed—

'it's *Escape from Darkness*, my very first film, and I nearly drowned, thanks to you!' She laughed and wept at the same time.

Radek whispered, 'It was silent, remember, so we put music to it.'

Blažena nodded, her heart too full for words. After all those films, and after all this time, she had not been forgotten. She was still loved.

END NOTES

For ease of reading, I have used English for the titles of the films referred to in the book. For those readers interested, the following list provides the English titles of the Czech films in order of reference, followed by their Czech titles.

Escape from Darkness: Útěk z Temnoty
Blue Diamond: Modry Demant
When the strings Shriek: Když struny Ikjí
The blue Light: Das blaue Licht
Enduring Love: Trvalá Láska
Wounded Heart: Zraněné Srdco
A Country Girl: Venkovská Dívka
Victory for the Country: Vítězství pro Vlast
The Wild Girl: Divoká Dívka
The Proud Princess: Pyšná Princezna
The Good Soldier Švejk: Dobrý Voják Švejk
Silent Barricade: Němá Barikáda
Silvery wind: Stribni Vitr